Forbidden West

Lucy Beena

Published by Red Letter Romance
Visit our website at www.RedLetterRomance.com
Red Letter Romance is an imprint of Elemental Ink Publishing LLC

Cover model images Copyright © VJ Dunraven Productions
Cover background image Copyright © Tomasz Zajda
Cover design by Kizmonster LLC

Paperback ISBN 979-8-88884-006-1
Hardcover ISBN 979-8-88884-007-8
Ebook ISBN 979-8-88884-008-5

First Edition November 2023

Forbidden West

Lucy Beena

RED LETTER
Romance

1880

Sierra Sutton

THERE WEREN'T many places to hide a gun while pretending to be a lady.

"You can't walk like that." Charity frowned as I hobbled across the rough wood floor.

"Like what?" I shifted my weight and kicked my foot at the heavy skirt. The dress fell all the way to the floor, and the neckline swept up to cover my normally exposed cleavage. I hadn't worn a dress this concealing since I was fifteen.

"Like you've got a six-shooter shoved up your coochie," Maggie stated.

"It's not shoved there," I mumbled. "And it's not a six-shooter."

"Pity," Maggie said. "Good place to keep one."

Charity covered her mouth to hide her laughter. Surely Maggie wasn't serious, but the woman had never cracked a joke in all the years I knew her.

"Maybe the gun isn't necessary," I said.

"'Course it is." Maggie grunted. You'd think Maggie was an old woman for all her bossing and grouching, but she was only ten years older than me. Though in the world of working girls, thirty-five was ancient.

"I don't even know how to use it." In fact, the gun made me nervous. Charity had strapped this one to my leg, so I hadn't even touched it. I'd only touched a gun once in my life and I didn't like to think about that night, or any of the nights that followed.

"Point and pull the trigger." I felt Maggie's eyes roll with her words.

I sighed. If only it was that easy.

"You probably won't even need it," Charity said. She smiled and it softened her features, making her look even younger than her eighteen years. I thought for the hundredth time how she didn't belong here. None of us did, but especially not Charity.

Maggie grunted at Charity's words but didn't say anything more. She shoved a few more items in my suitcase then thrust it toward me.

"If you plan on doing this, you'd better get to it." Maggie turned away before I could say anything and busied herself by fluffing the pillows on the bed and tugging at the sheets. She smacked the pillows roughly and dust drifted through the air. I thought I heard her sniff, but it was probably on account of all the dust in the air.

"Here," Charity held up my handbag. "All us girls contributed what we could. It's not much, but you shouldn't leave with nothin'." The purse was heavier than I'd ever felt it. I blinked away tears.

"I can't take these from you." I tried to give the bag back. The girls had nothing. Any coins they scrimped together didn't need to be wasted on me.

"You take those coins and make a new life for yourself, Sierra." Maggie's words were forceful, like she could fluff me the same way she'd manhandled the bed pillows.

"All of you deserve better lives." It was true. They deserved it as much as me.

"Everything comes in time," Maggie said. "I remember the day you came in clinging to your momma's skirts. Such a tiny thing, all dark curls and wide eyes. I knew you weren't meant for this life, and I wish I could've sent your momma away and told her to never look back, but I was too young and your momma too desperate. This is my chance to help you."

"Go on," Charity said. "You know you can't stay. Not with Preston hanging around all the time."

My shoulders tensed at the mention of the cattle baron's name. Preston didn't need to haunt my dreams. He haunted every night and waking hour of my life.

"But what if he hurts one of the other girls?"

"He's not the same with them," Maggie brushed away a strand of my hair then gently held my arm. I couldn't help wincing where she touched my hidden bruises. "Who knows why he acts the way he does, but it's only you that makes him crazy."

It seemed every man in the saloon had told me I made him crazy. Those were the only words I remembered from my one and only night with Jackson. The saloon owner had said he never had a girl that made him so crazy. So crazy he pulled out his pistol. No, I wouldn't think of that now, not when I was so close to escaping all of it.

"You just gotta put enough miles between you and this place before they realize you're gone." Maggie had been over this plan many times with me, but I was still nervous. I could take a beating from Jackson or Preston, but I couldn't stand it if they hurt one of the other girls because of me. Maggie pressed a piece of paper into my hand. It was worn and thin in my hand from the hours I'd spent folding and unfolding it. The hours I'd spent dreaming of a new life.

"You got a new man waiting for you, and he's gonna be good to you." Maggie looked into my eyes and her gaze was so hard and fierce, I could almost believe her words were true.

"I've never known a man like that," I whispered.

"But you will," Maggie said. Charity sighed and I imagined she was dreaming of finding herself such a man. I wondered for a moment if she should go instead of me. She was younger, better with children. She'd probably do a much better job of taking care of this man and his children than I would. But my body and heart still ached from last night with Preston, and for the first time in my life I felt a flare of hope. Hope that maybe something good would come my way for once. Hope that I did deserve a better life and maybe I would find it.

"I made a lot of men hard in my time, Sierra. After all those dicks, my heart was harder than any of them, but I care about you girls, and I want you to have a better life. You're in control now. Don't turn out like me. Don't let your past harden your heart."

I knew Maggie wanted me to find more than just a good life with the man I was going to work for, but I barely had hope in my heart. There wasn't any room for love. I would care for this man's children and his household, but if I never saw another dick in my life, it would be too soon. I'd spent enough time on my back to last me a lifetime, and the last thing I wanted to think about was inviting another man into my bed.

"I hope he's handsome," Charity giggled.

"He's probably old and crippled if he needs my help." I couldn't help being negative. The last thing I needed was them hoping for some kind of happily ever after. That's not what girls like me got.

"He's a widower," Maggie said. "With three kids that need a motherly figure, and they'll be lucky to have you."

"Well, it can't be any worse than the work I do here." I shifted nervously, and the gun dug into the tender flesh of my inner thigh.

"It could also be much better." Maggie kissed my cheek gruffly and spun me toward the window. "Out with you or you'll miss your train."

"Jackson knows you were with Preston last night, so he won't expect to see you 'til later," Charity said quietly.

I nodded. Everything was going to plan so far. Jackson was passed out drunk and would hopefully stay that way until my train was beyond the Missouri state line and well into Kansas. By the day after tomorrow, I would be in Colorado.

None of the saloon girls ever left. Jackson wouldn't see it coming. Once a girl worked for Jackson, she always worked for him. It didn't even cross his mind that any of us would be bold enough to go against him. Bold enough to leave.

Charity opened the window and I winced at the

loud creaking of the hinges. The alley was empty below, and it was too early for anyone to be lurking around the saloon.

I swung my leg out the window as Charity tied a rope to my suitcase handle. Maggie gripped my arm as I maneuvered over the ledge. A loud bang echoed from below, and I nearly lost my grip.

"What was that?" I panted with the effort of holding myself up.

Maggie opened her mouth to reply as a shout tore through the saloon.

"Charity!" Jackson's voice roared up the stairs and echoed off the walls.

2

Sierra

CHARITY FLINCHED and looked wildly at Maggie.

"Go on." Maggie jerked her head toward the door. "I can handle this."

Charity hurried out of the room, closing the door quietly so no one would hear which room she'd come from.

"This isn't going to work," I said.

"Don't start that now," Maggie ordered. "Everything will be fine. It's not too far to the ground. Lower yourself down and I'll help you get as close as you can." Maggie gripped my arms tightly as I dangled out the window. The ground felt far away, but I only fell a few feet when Maggie released me. I landed on my feet and reached up for my suitcase.

Maggie let the rope drop to the ground and I untied it from the handle. Then she dropped my handbag and parasol down and snapped the window shut.

I stood for a moment staring up, thinking Maggie might lean out one more time and give me one more piece of advice. One more piece of encouragement. But I knew the woman had spoken more this morning than she did in a whole week, and she'd probably already left my room and moved on to her morning chores.

She didn't have time for being sentimental, and neither did I.

I needed to catch my train, and I didn't want to hang around in the alley anyway. Anyone could walk by and see me standing here, and my new life would be over before it even got started.

The alley stunk to high heaven. I carefully stepped around the trash and dried vomit. I couldn't just look the part of a lady – I had to smell like it too. I certainly didn't want to show up at the train station reeking of a whorehouse back alley.

The sun beat down on me, and I was grateful for the small parasol Maggie had insisted I take. I didn't get out of the saloon much, so it felt like my face was on fire.

With the parasol shading me, I walked down the main road as confidently as I could. There hadn't been rain in days, and the road was hard-packed. The dry spell was unusual, and the small blessing bolstered the bubble of hope growing inside me. I could shake a little dust out of my clothes. Mud would have caused a much bigger mess.

I walked most of the way without seeing anyone. As I approached the train station, I paused at the number of people crowding the platform. Judging by the clock on the side of the station, I didn't have long to wait. I stuck to the edges of the crowd and tried to shield my face with the parasol. No one looked twice at me, but my stomach still churned. My hands were clammy with cold sweat.

At last, the ground rumbled with the coming of the train. I watched as steam billowed up from the horizon and then the engine came into view. I'd never been on a train before or even seen one this close. I could hear it from my room at the saloon, but hearing it and seeing it were very different. I unconsciously took a step back as the train chugged into the station and came to a stop. I bumped into a solid form behind me. I stepped away quickly and turned to apologize.

"I'm sorry, I –" Words failed me when I saw the familiar silver toed boots of Preston McKlellan. I didn't dare look up, but my eyes were drawn like a parched horse to water.

"No harm done," Preston scarcely looked at me. He tipped his hat and strode forward with the rest of the crowd boarding the train.

He didn't recognize me. I nearly laughed, and a bubble rose up in my chest. I clamped down on the emotion because if I started laughing now, I might never stop, and my hysterics would certainly draw his eye.

I knew I looked different in this dress, with my hair tucked under a bonnet, and without the makeup I usually wore, but I still couldn't process that Preston had barely acknowledged me. He had also been civil. That wasn't a side of him I was accustomed to seeing.

I took a deep breath and dug my ticket out of my purse.

This was it.

I was going to board this train and leave this town, and my life behind. Nerves and excitement twisted in my stomach. My hand shook as I held my ticket out to be punched.

"Welcome aboard, miss," the trainmaster tipped his hat. "Do you need help with your luggage?"

I hadn't expected the trainmaster to speak to me. I'm sure I stood there with my mouth open for far too long. Finally, I managed to stutter a reply, "No, no thank you. I can manage."

I hauled myself and my small suitcase up the steps

and onto the train. My heart was nearly beating out of my chest as I entered the second passenger car and found my seat. My eyes scanned the other seats quickly, but I didn't see Preston in this car. He was likely in first class.

"I can get that for you, miss," a man jumped up from his seat and reached for my suitcase. I flinched away from him but managed not to fall down.

"Sorry, you startled me." I tried to laugh away the way my body had reacted. "Thank you. Feels like I packed everything I own."

The man chuckled and heaved my luggage into the overhead bin.

I nearly collapsed into my seat and clutched my purse to keep from wringing my hands. I was so close to escape, but the train was still in the station. Out my window, all I could see was the road that would take me back to the saloon.

Just as the train whistled and the engine groaned with movement, the door to the car flew open with a bang.

I jumped in my seat, but I wasn't the only one startled by the sound. Everyone swiveled to look at the door as a figure ducked through.

My breath stopped in my chest. I could do nothing but stare at those blasted silver tipped boots as Preston strode into the aisle.

"Pardon, I went to the wrong car," he said with a

chuckle. From the answering giggles, I knew he'd turned his dimpled grin toward the other women in the car. I fiddled with my purse and tried to look busy as he strode past me and took a seat somewhere near the back of the car.

I looked out the window as the town disappeared. I tried to slow my breathing. I could do this. I would get to Colorado and Preston would be none the wiser. He probably wasn't going all the way to Colorado anyway. I tried to remember if he'd said anything last night that might give me a clue about where he was headed, but Preston wasn't much of a conversationalist. He'd said 'see you tomorrow night, honey' as he was tucking his dick in and leaving my room.

If he planned to see me tonight, he wouldn't be traveling far. Hopefully he was just going to the next town over, near the state line.

I breathed in slowly and tried to release some of the tension in my body. The gun pressed into my thigh when I shifted, and my breath caught. Could I really use that on someone? On Preston?

The feel of steel against my flesh helped ground me. I distracted myself by thinking through everything I knew about the man in Colorado. It wasn't much. What little I knew only served to stir my nerves again.

At least Preston was a known quantity. I didn't

know anything about this man in Colorado. He was a horse rancher and had three little ones. His wife was dead, and he needed someone to look after his home and children.

I would be working as a nanny, and that was all. If this man thought I'd be his next wife or keep his bed warm, I'd turn around and head right back to the saloon.

Still, that cursed little pocket of hope fluttered in my chest and made me believe everything would work out.

I needed a little hope in my life. I didn't have anything else.

Tucker West

IHADN'T BEEN into town in months. I tried to avoid coming in and usually just sent Clint, my ranch hand, to fetch supplies or run errands. My horse, Max, sensed my unease. He pawed at the ground and tossed his head.

"Easy, boy." I soothed him with a pat on his neck. He didn't care for town either. "Train should be in soon," I said to Clint.

"If it's on time," he replied.

"Does it run late often?"

Clint nodded.

I squinted at the horizon and held my hand up to measure the hours of daylight left.

"How late do you reckon it'll be?" We could still make it back to the ranch if the train was only an hour late.

"Depends," Clint shrugged. "I could check at the depot. See if they have any updates."

"No, just get our supplies. I'll go check."

"You sure? Remember what happened last time." I could see the amused glint in his eye. He was always up for trouble, especially if I started it. That's why he was my right-hand man. We had history together, and I knew he had my back.

"I'll play nice," I said. "Promise."

Clint laughed. "The day you play nice is the day daisies sprout from my head." He tugged the reigns of his horse and steered the wagon off the main road toward the general store.

"I'm always nice," I muttered to his back. That was partly true. I made an effort to be nice these days. I tried to set a good example for my children and live a life Mary would have been proud of. She had been the nice one. The calm one. And now, without her around, it took more effort to keep my cool. Especially when I came into town.

The depot was a shack at the end of the road. It

leaned too far to the left, and the porch was missing a step. The boards creaked under my feet as I pushed open the door and stepped inside. Light came in through two windows that faced the tracks. Dust hung in the air.

"Can I help you?" A stout man sat behind the sagging counter. He looked over the top of his glasses at me.

"Do you know what time the train from Cedar Pass will be in today?" I asked.

"Scheduled for 4:10 this afternoon."

"It's on time?"

"Didn't say that. Just said it's scheduled for 4:10."

I took a deep breath before carefully choosing my next words.

"I heard it might be late today. Do you have any updates?"

"I get updates sometimes but don't know if anything has come through today. Yesterday it was running about two hours off schedule."

I tried to tell myself the man wasn't being intentionally difficult. He was probably just stupid or lazy. Or both.

"You have a good day." I tipped my hat stiffly and stalked out of the shack.

Clint was waiting outside with a shit-eating grin on his face.

"Find yourself a helpful town person in there, did you?"

"Exceedingly helpful," I grumbled. "I'm headed to the hotel. Did you get the supplies?"

"The boys at the shop are loading them in the wagon." Clint walked beside me as I led Max down the street toward the only hotel in town. "I'll give everything a final count when they're done and settle the tab. There's a diner in the hotel."

"Good. Let's eat there, and then you can head back to the ranch," I said. Mrs. Grady from town was staying with the children while we were gone, but I didn't like for them to be without one of us there.

"Train running late?" Clint asked.

"I reckon." I still wasn't sure what time it would get in but guessed it would be at least two hours late based on the less than helpful depot man.

"Old Festus didn't have much to say on the matter?" Clint grinned.

"Festus, is that his name?" The old guy looked like a Festus.

"Well, you didn't resort to physical violence, so I'd call it a win," Clint said. "I've even wanted to punch ol' Festus in the face a couple times." He laughed and I couldn't help but smirk. Clint had been beside me through thick and thin, but he was a gentle soul deep down. I'd lost my anchor when Mary died a year ago, but Clint was the best friend I ever could have asked for. It wasn't the same, but without him and the kids, I would have lost myself. Lost myself to the person I was a long time ago. A person I never wanted to be again.

"You alright, boss?" Clint frowned at me, and I wondered how long I'd been standing still.

"I told you not to call me that." I walked away, and Clint followed.

Clint shrugged. "You wanting to go in there?" He jerked a thumb back toward the saloon we'd just passed.

"You know how I feel about those establishments."

"You was looking awful hard at something back there," Clint ribbed me.

"I was thinking," I said. "Didn't realize where we were."

"Reckon a visit with the proprietor might end your peaceful streak."

I could tell the idea of me beating the saloon owner to a pulp was the most exciting thing Clint could imagine happening on our trip into town.

"It might also end my no-killing streak," I said seriously.

"Some men are only good for killing." Clint spat a stream of tobacco juice in the direction of the saloon.

"I didn't come into town today to kill or maim or otherwise give myself a bad...worse reputation." After the fight a few months back, I already had some kind of reputation in town. I hoped this peaceful and uneventful outing would restore some goodwill with the town folk. Sending Clint to run all my errands was another way of building goodwill. Clint shared my background, but he could have been a politician. He always knew the exact right thing to say in a tense moment and could diffuse even the most explosive situations with his words.

I preferred diffusing situations with my six-shooter.

"Let's eat so you can go meet your new lady." Clint clapped me on the shoulder.

"She's not my lady," I growled. Clint had been playing matchmaker ever since I posted the ad for a caretaker for the children. "She's a nanny. Nothing more."

"Sure, whatever you say, boss." He pushed open the door to the hotel's diner.

I didn't care for Clint's insinuations. I'd tried to keep a professional outlook on the whole ad, but his continued chatter had me thinking. Mary was the only woman I ever really loved. Sure, I had my dalliances here and there, but Mary was the only one who had my heart. She was everything. I gave up everything for her, and I was happy. I didn't have any unrealistic expectations about the woman coming to work for me. She would be an employee just like Clint. Still, part of me hoped maybe she could be more than that.

I shook my head to dislodge these impractical thoughts. I scowled at Clint as I took a seat across from him. He just grinned.

"Got ya thinkin' now, huh, boss?" He chuckled.

"I told you not to call me that."

Sierra

PRESTON RODE the train longer than I expected. It was a relief to watch him disappear into a depot in Kansas. I hadn't realized how tense my whole body was until he was out of sight. I practically melted into the seat and fell asleep for the first time as soon as the train left that station.

The trip was much more enjoyable after my worry about Preston disappeared. I'd never felt so free in my life. The flat plains of Kansas turned into scrub brush, and then the gentle hills and green trees of Colorado. In the distance I could see the shadowed shapes of mountains. It was different from Missouri. Everything was greener.

The train made several stops along the way, and issues with refilling the water tanks caused delays. But now, the train arrived in Silver Springs, Colorado. After a brief moment of near euphoric freedom, all my nerves crashed down on me.

The train hissed to a stop at the station and passengers gathered their luggage. I stood to pull down my suitcase, but a man behind me hurried over to help.

"Let me get that, miss," he said.

I tried not to shy away from his proximity to me. I didn't know why this trip had made me so jumpy. In the saloon, I was always the best at working the crowd and keeping the men entertained. But here, out of my element and still sore from Preston's attentions, I felt like a fish out of water. I didn't know what these men expected or wanted from me. It was strange to have help offered and for me to give nothing in return.

"Thank you." I tried to smile at him when I took my suitcase, and I must have succeeded because he beamed at me and tipped his hat.

"You have a good day, miss," he said.

The depot platform was crowded with passengers boarding and deboarding the train, luggage on carts, and families squeezing in last-minute goodbyes. I skirted along the edge of the crowd and finally got off the platform to stand near the road.

I looked around, hoping my employer would find

me. I didn't know what he looked like, and he didn't know me, but surely there weren't that many single women arriving on this train. As the crowd thinned out and people disappeared onto the train or down the road with family in tow, I searched the remaining faces.

After dismissing several for various reasons, my eyes landed on a man astride a buckskin horse. He faced slightly away from me and was watching the platform, obviously looking for someone.

I didn't know much about the man I would be working for, other than his name, Tucker West, and that he had a horse ranch. Lots of people had horses though, so I couldn't say for sure if this was my future employer.

I was still staring when he turned his head. Our eyes met and my breath caught in my chest.

His eyes were dark as a moonless night. It wasn't just his eyes that sent a thrill through me. It was his strong jaw, his broad shoulders, and his chaps stretched tight over his thighs. He sat on his horse like a man who knew what he was about.

His whole being radiated strength.

Confidence.

Danger.

He dismounted his horse and walked toward me.

"Miss Sutton?" he asked.

I nodded dumbly. "Are you Tucker West?"

"I am." He smiled then, and I felt heat pool in my

stomach. I mentally admonished myself for swooning over a man I knew nothing about. I was never one to fall for a handsome face, and I wasn't about to start now.

"Let me get that for you." He reached across to take my suitcase. His arm met mine as I fumbled to hand the luggage to him.

I winced where he grazed my arm.

"Are you hurt?" He glanced down at my arm briefly before catching my eyes and holding them. I could fall into their depths, but I wouldn't.

"I'm fine, just sore from the long ride."

He gave a slow nod. I could tell he wanted to say something more, but he didn't. Those dark eyes spoke of hidden things. I imagined he wasn't a man who liked to share his secrets, so with any luck he wouldn't ask about mine.

"Is it far to your ranch?" I didn't know much about the man, but I knew he had a ranch and horses. I was ready to be away from crowds and get to work cleaning his house, feeding his children, and doing anything else to keep my nerves at bay.

"Not too far, but we won't make it before dark." He strapped my small suitcase to his horse where a saddlebag would normally go. "I sent my ranch hand home with the wagon and supplies earlier. We'll stay at the hotel and head out in the morning."

"Oh." I didn't mean to sound disappointed, but I must have, because he turned to look at me.

"Problem?"

"No, no problem, just eager to meet the children." And not stay in a hotel room with you. I refrained from wringing my hands and instead clutched my parasol until my knuckles turned white. I'd been counting on his children as a buffer. Surely he wouldn't try anything with them around, but if I was alone at a hotel with him, anything could happen. Maybe he didn't even have children, and this had been an elaborate ploy to get a woman he could have his way with. I felt my breath coming in gasps. There was really no reason for me to panic, but it was all too much.

I'd left everything and everyone I knew behind. I was in a strange town with a strange man and now I had to share a room with him.

I jumped at pressure on my elbow.

"Are you ok?" His eyes were clouded with worry, and his sun-drenched brow furrowed as he leaned in to look at me. His hand was on my elbow. Not hurting. Not squeezing. Just…holding. It was nice, but I still moved to smooth my skirts and break the contact.

"Yes, sorry, I must be more tired than I thought." I fanned myself even though I knew my movements were too erratic. Too nervous. "It's warm. I didn't expect Colorado to be so warm. I always heard about the snow."

"There's still some snow higher up in the mountains." He accepted the change in subject, and I was grateful. He turned his horse away from the depot and offered me his arm. "It's only a short walk to the hotel. Or you can ride Max if you're too tired."

He was offering to let me ride his horse. I would feel completely out of place if I rode his horse while he walked and led me through town. Whore on parade. The girls back home would get a kick out of that.

"No, no, I can walk." I cautiously hooked my hand in the crook of his elbow, and we set out toward the hotel. He didn't say anything more about my behavior and instead told me about his ranch and his horses. I appreciated the distraction and found his deep voice soothing. Standing so close, I felt the heat radiating off his body and the rumble of his words in his chest. His very broad chest.

I knew I shouldn't think about him like that. He'd been kind so far, but we were in public. Lots of men were nice in public. Even Preston was nice in public.

Behind closed doors, that's where men showed their true colors.

And this man might have a pretty face, but that didn't tell me anything about his heart.

I hadn't come all this way for a man's heart anyway. I'd come here for my heart. For a new life that didn't involve love or men of any kind.

Hard work and wrangling children, that's what I needed.

The only thing I needed.

Tucker

SIERRA SUTTON already had me in the palm of her hand, and I didn't even know her. I hadn't taken a full breath since my eyes met hers at the station. She was all soft curves and perfect lips, and I nearly lost myself when I looked at her. Her eyes were like bottomless pools and they swirled with a darkness I recognized.

I felt a sudden and overpowering sense of protectiveness.

I needed to take care of this woman.

Protect her.

The truth of this hit me in a way I couldn't explain, but I knew she needed me as much as I needed her. And I needed her in every way a man needs a woman, but I wouldn't think of all those ways now. She didn't need me horned up and lusting after her. I tried to think about anything else other than the soft woman on my arm.

Sierra was more skittish than a green-broke horse.

I wasn't an expert in the ways of women, but I had a way with the wildest horses, so I tried some of the same techniques. Not that I wanted to compare the woman to a horse, but talking about the weather and moving slowly calmed all God's creatures.

She was nervous, but I wasn't sure why. It seemed like more than just anxiety about being in a new place with me, a man she didn't know. She was nervous at the station, but when I mentioned staying in town, her whole body tensed, and she went pale as a sheet. I worried she would pass out.

As far as I knew, she was new to this town. She didn't have any enemies here, but if anyone knew about enemies it was me. There probably wasn't a town west of the Mississippi unaware of Tucker West, and in each place someone there would shoot me as soon as look at me. Lucky for me, I was a quick draw with a deadly aim.

But I'd left all that behind and started a new life with Mary and the kids.

Mary.

What would she think of me now?

What would she think of Sierra?

It had been a year, but sometimes if felt like a month, a week…a day. Sometimes I thought if I turned my head fast enough, I could catch her coming in from the garden. If I stretched out my hand, I might feel her warmth beside me in bed. I shook my head to clear those thoughts. The grief came in waves most days, and this wasn't a day I wanted to be sucked under the surface.

"There's a diner at the hotel," I said. We were nearly to the hotel now, but had to walk past the saloon. I've known some decent saloons in my travels, but this was not such an establishment.

If I could, I would burn it to the ground.

"Evening, Tucker," a voice called from the porch of the saloon.

"Sheriff." I tipped my hat. Sheriff Tuff Hale was the best lawman I knew and an old friend. "Trouble?"

"Just keeping an eye on things." He looked toward the door where the saloon owner, Harlan, was having a tense discussion with another man. Tuff was good about looking out for the girls, but he could only do so much. He couldn't help what went on behind closed doors. Not unless the girls came to him and made a report, which they never did.

Sierra tensed at my side. Her fingers dug into my arm near my elbow. I looked at her. Her eyes were riveted on the saloon and the men in the doorway.

"We best be on our way," I said to Tuff. "Good to see you."

"You too. You should come around more often, Tucker. Don't forget that offer I made you."

I chuckled. "I haven't forgotten. The answer's still no but come out to the ranch sometime. The kids would love to see you."

"I'll do that." He tipped his hat to Sierra.

Sierra's steps were wooden beside me as I guided her past the saloon. I pointed out some other buildings across the street and finally pulled her attention back to me.

"The Mercantile has the best selection of hard candy west of the Mississippi. We'll have to get some in the morning before we leave. I would say it's for the kids, but I love the peppermint sticks."

"Oh, I've never had any," Sierra said.

"Peppermint sticks?"

"Candy." She blushed and it was like a sunset over the desert - her eyes dark as night, her skin like the warm sand and that blush like the setting sun.

"Well, then it'll be my treat. We'll get whatever you want in the morning." If I thought her blush was lovely, it was nothing like her smile. For the first time since I collected her from the train station, she smiled at me, and it was like looking at the sun.

"Here we are." I tied Max to the post outside, then opened the hotel door and motioned Sierra ahead of me.

She was nervous again. Her hands clenched her parasol and purse with a white-knuckled grip.

"I'll need my horse stabled for the night, and I've already made reservations for two rooms."

Sierra jerked her head toward me. Surprise on her features. I frowned, unsure what caused that reaction.

"Of course, sir, and will you need anything else?" The desk attendant was the most competent person in town so far.

"The lady will take dinner in her room." I turned to Sierra, "Unless you prefer to eat in the diner?"

She looked toward the dining area, crowded with families and loud men. She shook her head.

"The room...my room is fine," she said. "Thank you."

"Your keys, sir." The attendant passed me two keys. I handed one to Sierra. "I'll have dinner sent up within the hour, miss. Tonight's special is fried chicken and potatoes."

Sierra nodded stiffly. I resisted the urge to guide her to her room. I picked up her suitcase and my satchel and headed for the stairs. I didn't want to push her, but I wanted her to follow and finally relax in her room.

I heard her steps behind me on the stairs. When I looked back, she was clutching the key like her life depended on it. Maybe it did. I didn't know what her story was or where she came from, but I wanted her to trust me.

"Here you go." I set her suitcase down in front of a door and nodded to the one across the hall. "I'll be right there. If you need anything, just knock."

"You got me my own room?" She seemed to be searching my eyes for something.

I was confused by her words. "Of course. It's the proper thing to do."

She murmured something that sounded like 'proper' and laughed under her breath.

"I'd like to leave early tomorrow, but we're not in a big hurry. Clint will have things under control at the ranch, and Mrs. Grady is watching the children."

"You already have a nanny?" Now she was the one looking confused.

"No, Mrs. Grady just watches the children every now and then, when I'm gone overnight or Clint and I are both away for the day. She's older, so watching the kids more than once a month is more than she can handle."

"Of course. Sorry, I shouldn't pry." She fiddled with the key in her hands.

"No apology necessary. You're welcome to ask about anything. I'll let you get some sleep and see you in the morning. Can't leave town without our candy."

She seemed to relax at that and smiled before slipping into her room. I heard the lock click into place then went into my own room. I debated kicking off my boots and stretching out on the bed, but it was still early. The sun was just setting outside, and I knew Tuff would still be at the sheriff's office. It would be good to catch up with my old friend.

He was good at keeping me out of trouble, too.

Usually.

Sierra

I STARED AT MY door for a long while after closing and locking it.

I heard Tucker go into his own room, but he left only a few minutes later. I didn't like to think about where men went and what they did after dark, and I didn't like to think that Tucker might be one of those men.

A knock at my door startled me.

My heart pounded in my chest but then a soft voice said, "Room service."

I opened the door and a young woman held out a wooden tray laden with food and beverage.

"Your dinner, miss. Would you like me to set it on the table?"

"No, no that's fine, I can take it. Thank you." I took the tray and nudged the door shut with my foot. I made sure to lock it again once I'd set the food down. If someone really wanted to get in, they could kick the door in, but at least no one would be sneaking up on me. I hadn't been allowed to lock my door at the saloon. Just knowing I had that control here relaxed me in a way I had never known.

The table was set near the window. I pulled back the curtain to see outside. It was dark, but the street lanterns were lit. I could see people walking along the street and riding horses and wagons. I had always liked to watch people from my window at the saloon. I liked imagining their lives and what it would be like to have a life like that. I cracked open the window and let the cool night breeze ruffle my hair.

I caught snippets of conversations as people walked by the hotel while I ate my dinner. Then, loud voices drew my attention. Men were arguing. I strained to see where the voices were coming from, and my breath caught in my throat when I saw a group of men outside the saloon.

Tucker was there.

Breathe. Just because he was there, it didn't mean anything. Some men played cards or drank. Surely he wasn't going for the women...but he's a widower. Of course, he would be lonely. Some men treated the girls nice. I never knew any men like that, but the other girls had gentle lovers sometimes. Quiet, lonely men that wanted something warm and soft, even if just for one night. Not men like Preston that needed control and just wanted to take, take, take.

I pressed a hand to my chest. My heart raced and my breath came in short gasps.

I shook my head and focused on the scene below.

Tucker and the sheriff were with three other men and one of the saloon girls. One of the men was yelling. He was thinly built with a goatee and sandy-colored hair that hung past his shoulders. I realized I hadn't heard Tucker's voice yet. They were all standing outside; maybe he hadn't actually gone into the saloon.

"Think you're better than the rest of us, do ya?" the thin man shouted.

"Easy, Harlan. We don't want any trouble." The sheriff tried to soothe the riled man.

"That one there, he always wants trouble." Harlan pointed at Tucker.

"Not tonight. We were just concerned about the lady." The sheriff motioned to the girl standing beside Harlan. She was looking away from the men, one hand crossed in front of her to hold her other arm. She might have looked bored to most people, but I knew she was trying to make herself as small as possible. Trying not to be seen. That was all a saloon girl thought about – when to be seen and when to be nothing but a shadow. When men started arguing, nothing good came.

"The lady?" Harlan laughed, but it was a harsh, cruel sound. "That ain't no lady and she ain't no concern of yours anyway. Get inside, Marla."

I stiffened at his words and pulled away from the window. No one could see me — I was certain. Still, I didn't want any of these men to catch me eavesdropping. I leaned next to the window with my back against the wall. I could still hear the voices and easily recognized who was talking.

"The lady was calling for help," Tucker said. "She didn't want the company of these men."

"She'll go with whoever pays for her company. Get inside, Marla!" Harlan shouted. I heard a rustle and a scuffling of feet.

At the sound of a cocked gun, I froze. My breath left my body, and a chill ran through me. It was silent outside, so I peeked around the curtain to see what was happening.

Harlan gripped Marla's arm as she cowered beside him. The other men stood still, and Tucker...Tucker had his pistol pointed at Harlan's head.

"Easy boys," the sheriff said. "Harlan, let go of Marla, and Tucker, holster your shooter."

"You gonna shoot me over a whore?" Harlan said,

but his words didn't carry the same gusto as before.

"I don't need a reason to shoot you," Tucker said. "You just make it easier when you give me a reason by disrespecting the lady."

His voice was deep and dark and full of dangerous things. My heart swelled with a feeling I didn't recognize. Tucker was defending a woman, and not just any woman. A working girl. A girl like me.

"That's not me anymore," I said quietly. I wasn't like Marla anymore, but I could have been.

I had been.

Tucker lowered his pistol and Harlan released Marla. The girl picked herself up and scurried away into the saloon. I wondered what kind of backlash she would face over the night's events.

I wondered what kind of backlash Tucker would face too, though he didn't seem like a man who cared what the consequences were. I watched him as the men dispersed. Even at this distance, in the dancing lantern light, I could see the dark intensity of his gaze. His form was rigid, his hand still resting on the hilt of his pistol.

I'd never seen a man look as good as Tucker did in that moment, and it scared me. I wasn't supposed to find this man attractive. I wasn't supposed to even think about him in ways that made my heart race.

I pulled away from the window and tugged the curtains closed. The excitement was over, even if my heart was still racing. I didn't know if it would ever slow down now that Tucker West was in my life.

Tucker didn't say anything about the previous night's events when I met him for breakfast. The diner was nearly empty. I was grateful for the quiet, though it didn't give me much in the way of distractions. I pushed my food around on my plate and tried to eat, but my nerves still thrummed. I started to ask Tucker how his evening went more than once, but I didn't want to hear him lie to me. I don't know why, but I was certain he wouldn't tell me what happened. I had this image of him now, and I didn't want to spoil it.

"Saving room for candy?" Tucker asked. His voice was gentle, almost teasing. He looked pointedly at my plate.

I laughed, grateful for the proffered excuse. "You caught me."

"Just in case candy isn't enough, I'll hold onto these for the ride home." He took the last two biscuits from the basket and wrapped them in a clean handkerchief. Then he tucked them in his satchel.

The morning was crisp and the breeze cool. As we walked to the Mercantile, I was grateful for my dress with long sleeves. Of course, all my dresses had long sleeves now. Not that I was complaining. My dresses felt like shields, a way to hide myself and my past. A past I didn't want to think about but had left my arms mottled with bruises. I didn't need Tucker or anyone else asking questions about how I got them. They were just bruises, and with any luck, they'd be gone in a week.

Tucker held the door open for me. The bell overhead chimed as we entered.

The man behind the counter greeted him. "Mornin', Mr. West."

Tucker nodded to the man. "James, I told you to call me Tucker."

"Of course," James chuckled. "What can I get for you and the missus today?"

I blushed furiously at the man's insinuation. I felt Tucker's hand at the small of my back. His touch was so light I felt barely more than the heat of his hand. I met his eyes and was surprised to see amusement twinkling in their depths. I glared at him. His lips curled in a small smirk before he turned back to James.

"This is Sierra. She's coming to work as a nanny for the children."

"Apologies. I didn't mean to imply."

Tucker shrugged. "No harm done. We're here for some candy. I'd say it's just for the kids, but you know I never can tell a lie."

James chuckled and moved over to stand behind the glass cabinet where jars and jars of candies were displayed. I stood back as Tucker made his selections. I'd never been to the general store in Missouri. Some of the girls had regulars that would bring them little sweets, but I never did. If I had candy as a child, I didn't remember.

Tucker turned toward me, a small smile on his face. But when he met my eyes, his smile faltered. I tried to school my features, wondering what he saw that gave him pause. Longing for a life I should have had? A childhood I missed? I shook myself mentally and tried to focus on the candy. I smiled, probably too brightly.

He stepped closer, and I was intensely aware of our height difference. He towered over me. He was taller than Preston. I brushed thoughts of that man out of my mind. Tucker was nothing like him. I had to believe that.

Tucker nodded his head toward the candy display. His voice was soft. "Get whatever you want."

"I don't even know what I'd like," I whispered.

"I'll give you a hint." Tucker leaned toward me. I felt his words as much as I heard them. "Everything's delicious."

I tried not to fidget. Tried to calm my nerves. Tried to look like I belonged here. Like I was just a regular person out shopping.

And I was. The thought hit me suddenly.

I was safe here with Tucker. I was a lady with him. A nanny, and no one saw me as anything other than that. No one knew where I came from or what I was. What I had been. I'd played my part at the saloon, wooing men I had no interest in wooing. Playing the seductress. This was just a different role. One I was unfamiliar with, but I could learn. I could play this part for now. Maybe someday it wouldn't feel like a part. Maybe someday it would feel real.

I smiled at the thought and a spark of confidence flared inside me for the first time since I'd stepped off the train in Colorado. If Tucker noticed the change in me, he said nothing. I felt his eyes watching me as I stepped up to the counter.

"I'm afraid I can't make up my mind." I smiled at James and laughed a little at myself, as if this was a common occurrence. As if I went to the store every day of the week.

"Then maybe one of each," James said with a wink.

"Oh." I glanced over my shoulder and saw Tucker chuckling.

"Give her whatever she wants," he said.

"For the children of course," I said to James.

"Of course." He laughed and bagged up the candy. The brown paper sack was nearly bursting when he finished.

Tucker paid and we strolled back out into the cool morning.

"We'll leave Max at the stable and borrow Mrs. Grady's horse and wagon. Clint will bring Mrs. Grady back to town later today and ride Max home," Tucker said as we walked back to the hotel. "Ask the bellman to help you with the luggage. I'll get the wagon ready."

Despite Tucker's words, I didn't want to ask for help. But I also knew I'd never seen a lady lugging her own suitcase around town.

The man at the front desk spoke as I approached. "Good morning, Miss. How can I help you?"

"We're checking out, and I need someone to bring down my luggage."

"I'll send someone right up," he said.

It was easy. I couldn't believe how good it felt to just ask for something and receive help, with no expectation of giving something in return. Well, other than a tip.

I hurried up the stairs with the keys to our rooms. I grabbed Tucker's satchel from his room first and set it in the hallway, then I quickly packed my suitcase. That blasted pistol was still strapped to my leg. It chafed something awful, but I was too nervous to touch it. I decided to worry about it when we got to the ranch.

The bellman arrived to help with the luggage, and I followed him down the stairs. I tipped him when we reached the entrance to the hotel. Tucker was just outside the door. He had the horse and wagon waiting, so I stepped outside. I opened my mouth to ask him to come help when I realized he wasn't alone.

The men from last night surrounded him.

The sheriff was nowhere in sight.

Tucker

HARLAN WAS an idiot. He and two of his
lackeys thought we had unfinished business.
He didn't know me very well.
I never left business unfinished.

"Where you goin', cowboy?" Harlan hollered.
His face really was the type that begged to have a fist put
through it. Or a bullet.

I didn't let these sorts of men get to me anymore,
though. Calmness always infuriated hotheads like them.
They couldn't plan farther than they could piss, so it was
easy to maintain the upper hand. It didn't matter that they

outnumbered me. I had six bullets in my gun, and I only needed three... if it came to that.

And I really hoped it did.

Harlan was a plague upon this town, and I welcomed a reason to exterminate him.

"I asked you a question," Harlan snarled again.

He might be able to intimidate the ladies in his saloon and the sniveling men beside him, but I knew lots of men like Harlan. He didn't scare me.

I finished adjusting the horse's harness and turned to him with a smirk. "I might ask you the same thing."

Tuff wasn't around, so I thought maybe I should try to play nice. Besides, I had Sierra to think about now and she was coming out of the hotel any minute. Somehow, I knew this situation would do nothing for her nerves. She was such a jumpy thing, and aside from finally showing some spunk in the mercantile, she didn't need to catch me flogging three of the town idiots.

"You think I'd let you leave town after last night?" Harlan said.

"I'm a sucker for damsels in distress." I shrugged and gave him my most disarming smile. "What can I say, women do that to me."

"You need to mind your own fucking business, and I aim to help you remember that." Harlan motioned for his men to come closer.

"What's the plan here, gentleman?" I stood with

my thumbs hooked in my belt. My feet were planted wide and my posture at ease. I knew I looked relaxed, careless even, but inside I was wound tight as an iron spring. I hoped Tuff might show up and keep me from doing something stupid. I certainly wouldn't regret it, but it *would* be something stupid.

I heard the hotel doors open behind me. A feminine gasp drew my attention.

Well, shit.

Sierra stood on the porch, eyes wide, staring at me and the unfolding drama. Her chest rose and fell with her quick breaths. I couldn't help staring at the way her breasts strained against the cotton dress even as I wondered if she might faint.

I turned my attention back to the men. I couldn't afford to be distracted, especially now that Sierra's safety might be at risk.

"What's this?" Harlan narrowed his eyes and looked between me and Sierra. "Didn't know you had a woman, cowboy."

"How about we just forget last night and go our separate ways?" It was a generous offer. As much as I wanted to stay and play this little game of cat and mouse, I didn't want Sierra to end up in the middle of anything. I was also trying to build a new reputation for myself, and so far, I was doing a bang-up job. At least I'd managed to keep my gunfighting skills under wraps. A fist fight and a few verbal disagreements here and there didn't cause nearly the same ruckus as a full-on shootout.

And this little confrontation had all the signs of a shoot-out.

It seemed I wasn't the only one that felt the signs of a standoff. There hadn't been many people on the streets this morning, but now I noticed there were even fewer, and most had gone indoors to observe from behind doors and windows. Shopkeepers closed the shutters over their glass windows. Guess it never hurt to be cautious. Windows were expensive, and I imagined Harlan and his men were lousy shots.

The men were jumpy. Their hands hovered over their gun belts. Not quite close enough to be a direct threat, but near enough to be impolite. Their intention was clear. Whether they intended to hold a gun on me while Harlan got some licks in or they would actually shoot me, was yet to be determined. Of course, I didn't plan to find out.

I would let them make the first move, but it would be their last.

"Haven't seen you around, girl," Harlan shouted toward Sierra. "What's a pretty thing like you doing with this goat roper?" He laughed at his own joke and the men laughed with him.

"She's not part of this. If you have something say, say it to me."

"I'll say whatever I want to whoever I want,

cowboy. It's time you learned you don't call the shots in this town." Harlan nearly spat the words at me. He shifted his attention back to Sierra, and hot anger boiled up in my chest like a blacksmith's forge. "A pretty thing like you needs a real man. Ain't that right, boys? Bet I'd give you the best night of your life, darlin'. Anybody ever fuck those tits?"

I took two steps and clocked Harlan in the jaw. He collapsed like a puppet whose strings got cut. He only lay still for a moment before he started thrashing. His men rushed over to help him up.

Someone grabbed my arm and I turned quickly, my mind searching for threats, but the hand was small, the grip weak.

Sierra.

She shrank away from me, and I wondered what she saw in my face.

"I'm sorry," I murmured. "We should go."

She nodded quickly. While the men were still getting Harlan back on his feet, I helped Sierra into the wagon. Her waist felt impossibly small in my hands and despite the urgency I felt, I couldn't help but wonder at the softness of her. Once she was up, I grabbed the two bags from the porch steps quickly and tossed them into the back of the wagon.

I came around to climb in beside Sierra but stopped short at the shotgun aimed at my gut.

Where Harlan's man had gotten a shotgun was beyond me. I cursed myself for not knocking out all of them. I was sure my punch should have dropped Harlan, but the man had a thicker skull than I expected. Or maybe I was just out of practice. I had planned on his goonies backing off if he was out cold, but now he was back on his feet and staggering toward the wagon.

"Oh, you've really done it now, cowboy." Harlan's words slurred a bit, and I held out hope that he might still pass out. He took a step toward Sierra. I moved to intercept him, but the guy with the shotgun jabbed it into my side.

"Now, are you gonna come down here and be a good girl while we teach your man a lesson in how a woman ought to be treated?" Harlan laughed. The look in his eyes was deadly.

Sierra sat ramrod straight on the bench. Tension and fear radiated from her body, but I was surprised by the fire in her eyes as she glared down at Harlan.

I could take these three, but I worried what Sierra would think of me. I couldn't gun down three men in the street without consequences.

I'd really fucked this all up.

Harlan reached for Sierra and caught her wrist. I took another step toward them, but Snaggletooth hit me in the gut with the shotgun. The air went out of me as I watched Harlan drag Sierra down from the wagon and pull her close to him.

"Let's see what you're hiding under all these clothes," Harlan said. Sierra struggled against him and fell. He reached for her wrist again and her sleeve fell back as he grabbed her. "What's this?"

Sierra struggled harder as Harlan turned her hand over to look at something on the inside of her wrist. She was like a wildcat caught in a snare. She looked at me and then looked away. Her eyes were wild with fear and panic.

Harlan laughed.

"Ho boy, lookee here, cowboy been holdin' out on us," he said. He wrenched Sierra's arm to show the other two what he was looking at. A small brand shaped like a playing card marred the delicate skin of her wrist. An ace of spades. "You're just too good for our whores, cowboy, is that it? Had to get one of your own?"

Harlan released Sierra's wrist and she snatched her arm away. She backed away but was caught between Harlan and the wagon.

"Oh, you didn't know, did you? Well, that is rich." Harlan laughed again. I was really getting tired of that sound. "You got yourself an Ace in the Hole whore, and I reckon Jackson will be wantin' her back. Nobody leaves Hole House. Ain't that right, girl?" Harlan ran his hand along Sierra's face, his fingers trailing along her neck, but as his hand started past her shoulder the smoldering fire of rage inside me was stoked to a roaring furnace.

I turned and knocked the shotgun away from me. It went off with a crack and the buckshot kicked up dirt in the street. I drew my pistol in the same moment. The echo of the shotgun muted the report of my shot. Snaggletooth went down with a cry, his hands gripping his busted knee. I heard him fall to the ground, his agonized cries like a dying hog, but my focus was back on Harlan.

I leveled my pistol at him.

"Get away from her." My words were harder than the steel of my pistol.

"You shot Bomey!" Harlan's eyes darkened with rage, but I could see a flicker of fear there as well. He clearly had expected his three-on-one strategy to go off without a hitch. He looked between Sierra and me, trying to decide on his next move. He tightened his grip on Sierra, and I drew back my hammer.

The remaining man shifted. I drew my other gun on him.

Nobody moved.

A shot echoed in the street, and everyone flinched.

"What seems to be the problem, gentlemen?" Tuff's voice boomed down the street. I glanced and saw him on the back of a black steed, his gun drawn and still raised where he had fired a shot into the air. His deputies were mounted on horses on either side of him, shotguns in hand, the hilts resting on their thighs.

I stared at Harlan, and he stared at me.

"This isn't over, cowboy," he said, his words not loud enough for Tuff to hear. He released his grip on Sierra and stepped away. "Just a little misunderstanding, sheriff. Little misfire. You know how those shotguns are sometimes, sticky trigger and shaky trigger fingers." He plastered a fake smile on his face.

I could tell Tuff wasn't buying any of it, but if we could all walk away, no one would raise a fuss about any of today's events.

"Is that how it was?" Tuff looked at me. I could tell he was hoping I would give him an excuse to throw Harlan in a cell, but I was the only one who had actually shot anyone. If Harlan was willing to play this game, then so was I.

"Yes, sir, just a little misunderstanding. No hard feelings." There were hard feelings. And I knew this wouldn't be the last I saw of Harlan and his gang. Just one more reason to stay away from town.

I holstered my gun and moved to Sierra's side in two steps. Her body trembled, but her face was set in a hard line. Her eyes shone, though I could tell she wasn't going to cry here. I wouldn't have cared, but I admired her fierceness. A new heat pumped through my veins, and this had nothing to do with anger. I wanted to know more about this fierce yet fragile woman.

I wanted to know everything about her.

Tuff rode over to us as his deputies kept an eye on Harlan. He and the other man helped the one I shot. They dragged him over to the barbershop, likely looking for a quick fix even though there was a perfectly good doctor down the road. Of course, the doctor was a woman, and I doubted the men wanted anything to do with her.

Tuff dismounted his horse and eyed Sierra. "Are you okay, Miss?"

She nodded, but I could see her fierce facade melting before my eyes. She looked away and then started to wring her hands before settling for gripping them together tightly.

Tuff looked like he wanted to say more, and maybe offer help, but I shook my head slightly. I imagined the best thing for Sierra, for both of us really, was to get back to the ranch.

"Take care of yourself, Tucker." Tuff shook my hand. "I'll swing by the ranch in a couple days." Then he tipped his hat to Sierra and rejoined his deputies.

"Here, let me help you up so we can get out of here." I lifted Sierra up into the wagon again, this time noticing how she trembled in my grip. I hated Harlan for doing this to her, but I hated myself too. I shouldn't have let it get that far.

Next time, I'd shoot them all.

Sierra

I COULDN'T STOP shaking. It wasn't the first time I had seen men fight. It wasn't the first time a man grabbed me the way Harlan did. And I heard far more disgusting words courtesy of Preston and every other man who stepped through the doors of Jackson's Saloon. I didn't know why the whole thing left me in such a state.

Or maybe I did.

I glanced at Tucker, but the man was stoic as ever. He didn't say a word after we left town. The muscle in his jaw twitched as he clenched his teeth.

My fingers worried the sleeve of my dress where it covered the brand I received at age fifteen. The brand marking me as the property of Jackson.

An ace of spades.

I hated it. And I hated that Tucker had seen it. Everyone in town had probably seen it.

They knew what I was — what I had been. And Tucker did too. My new life was over before it even started. I couldn't imagine he wanted me around his kids now.

I couldn't stand the silence and the worry that the other shoe would drop at any moment.

"I'm sure I could catch a train back tomorrow." I hated that my voice sounded small.

Tucker whipped his head to look at me. Confusion showed on his face.

"You won't want me to look after your kids now that you know I..." I couldn't finish the thought. I wouldn't call myself a whore, even if that's what I was.

He relaxed a bit and turned back to the trail ahead. "None of that matters. You came here for a job, and if you still want it, it's yours."

I watched him, searching for signs of deceit. Maybe he was hoping I was more willing to jump in his bed since he knew something about my past. I narrowed my eyes, a sudden burst of anger flaring in my chest.

"I'm here for the job and nothing more."

He looked at me again, confusion once more clouding his eyes as he worked through my words.

"Of course. I don't know what else..." His eyebrows raised with understanding, but then his eyes hardened. "I don't expect anything else." He snapped the reigns a little harder than seemed necessary, and the horse picked up the pace. His jaw ticked even more than it had earlier. If I thought the silence was tense before, it was nearly suffocating now.

The wagon bumped along the rocky road as we wound up and down the narrow mountain passes. Wildflowers dotted the grassy hillsides. Red stones jutted from the ground like a giant's fingers. The air cooled as we went up the mountain, and I wondered when winter would arrive. It had been so warm in town the day before that I had given little thought to the passing season. I took in a deep breath, savoring the cool but not cold air, and let it out with a sigh. I finally stopped shaking.

I felt Tucker shift on the seat beside me. When I looked at him, I was surprised to find him watching me.

"Are you okay?"

"I'm fine, just enjoying the mountain air." I smoothed my skirt over my thighs. I tugged at my sleeve again. Tucker's eyes followed my movements, his gaze lingering on my arm where the brand was covered.

"I mean, are you okay after what happened in town?" His voice was soft and deep. It rumbled through me, and I unconsciously clenched my thighs together. The pistol that was still strapped there dug into the tender skin and I winced. I looked away quickly, hoping Tucker hadn't seen, but of course, this man saw everything.

"What's wrong? Are you injured?" His eyes scanned me from head to toe, looking for the source of my discomfort.

"I'm fine, just sore from all this travel." I didn't mean to sound so irritable, but I didn't want to talk about the bruises on my body, the gun strapped to my leg, or the pain that wasn't entirely from the holster chafing my tender skin.

"You said that yesterday too," he said.

"And it's just as true today as yesterday." I looked away from him, squinting at the horizon and trying to appear terribly interested in the scenery.

He was quiet for a while, and I thought he had finally taken the hint. The wagon hit a rut in the road, and I bounced in my seat. I landed with a squeak and couldn't help reaching for his arm to steady myself. My back and bottom landed hard against the wooden seat and I closed my eyes to keep in the tears that had sprung to my eyes.

Tucker reigned in the horse and the wagon stopped.

His arm was solid under my hands. I felt his warmth even through the flannel shirt he wore. I pulled my hands away quickly and adjusted myself on the bench.

"Sorry," I said. "That bump caught me by surprise."

"Nothing to be sorry about," Tucker said. I thought he would tell the horse to go, but he didn't. I squirmed in my seat, not looking at him. "There's a doctor in town."

"I don't think we'd be too welcome back in town right now, and I don't need another man fussing over me." I never liked the doctor that came around Ace in the Hole. Jackson always insisted on being in the room to make sure we behaved and didn't talk about him, but it didn't matter anyway. The doctor was there to collect coin and nothing more. He didn't care why girls needed stitches, he just did the stitchin'.

"It's a woman."

"What?"

"The town doctor is a woman, and she makes house calls," he said.

"Oh," I had nothing to say to that, and some of the bluster went out of my sails.

Tucked flicked the reins and clicked his tongue, and the horse started walking again. The wagon jolted into motion, but I held onto the seat this time instead of his arm. Even though part of me really wanted an excuse to hold his arm again. I shook my head. No. I couldn't think like that. He seemed nice, but I had seen him in the street. The look in his eye. This man was dangerous, and I knew what happened to women who got close to dangerous men.

But I could work for him. I could take care of his children and stay out of his way.

"Doctor's due to come out anyway," Tucker said as if he was talking about the weather. I resisted rolling my eyes but didn't look at him. "My youngest fell off a horse last week and needed a few stitches. Doc said she'd come out to remove the stitches. She has some other house calls to make out past the ranch."

I couldn't work out why he was worrying himself over me seeing the doctor, unless he was worried I wouldn't be able to do my job. That had to be it.

"I'm fine and nothing's gonna keep me from taking care of your kids and the house and doing the cooking." The only thing I was really worried about was the cooking, but that was because I'd never done it before.

Tucker frowned, and I wonder if he was as confused by me as I was by him.

"You think I'm asking you to see the doctor 'cause I'm worried you can't work?"

This man. "Well, I don't know why else you'd be worrying about it."

"I just don't want you hurtin'. I thought maybe the doc could help," he said.

My mouth fell open, but I quickly snapped it shut. "And what about you?" I asked.

"What about me?"

"You took a pretty hard hit from that guy you shot. You gonna let the doctor look at your ribs?" Two could play this game.

"I'm fine," he grunted. "I've had worse."

"So have I." As soon as the words were out of my mouth, I knew it was the wrong thing to say.

"That doesn't make me feel any better."

"I'm fine," I said through clenched teeth. This man was infuriating and intense, and I hated that he made my heart flutter. He barely knew me, and yet he had shown me more consideration than any man in my entire life.

Tucker eased the wagon to a stop and climbed down. We were in a flat, grassy area with a small stream running not far from the road.

"Let's take a break and try some of that candy," he said. I was grateful for the change of subject and the break. The candy wasn't a bad idea, either. I couldn't help smiling at him and didn't mind the way his hands felt around my waist when he gently helped me from the wagon. "I have some real food, too. Reckon we can't just eat candy."

His breath was warm against my ear as he lowered me to the ground.

"We could." I smiled, and my breath caught when he smiled back.

"We certainly could." He chuckled a bit, then stepped away quickly as if he hadn't realized how close we were. He went to the horse and unhooked her from the wagon. He spoke softly to her and scratched behind her ears ,then gently pulled out the twigs that had tangled in her mane. He tied her out where she could graze and drink from the stream.

Tucker opened one of the bags of candy and tossed me a green and white striped piece. I caught it and turned it over in my hands.

I wanted to believe this was the kind of good man Maggie spoke of, but it was hard to trust. Hard to trust a man, but hard to trust myself too. I was fooled once. I wouldn't be fooled ever again.

Still, I didn't squash the tiny fluttering of hope that stirred in my chest.

Tucker

I WAS EAGER to be home and see the kids, but I didn't want this ride with Sierra to end. I liked being close to her, feeling her softness beside me even if she was wound tighter than a banjo string. I probably shouldn't have mentioned the doctor, but I was worried about her. Especially now that I knew where she came from. I hadn't heard of Ace in the Hole, but it didn't sound like an upstanding establishment if the women were branded like cattle.

Just the thought of that sent liquid rage pumping through my veins. I reckoned my teeth would be worn down to nubs from the tension in my jaw. It was giving me a headache. What I really wanted to do was turn the wagon around, drag Harlan into the street, and shoot him like the dog he was, but that wasn't going to happen. Today anyway. I wouldn't rule it out for the future.

I could tell Sierra was sore from more than just travel, but she was stubborn and determined to hide from me. I could only hope she would talk with the doctor when she came to check on Tuck Jr.

I smiled at the thought of my youngest. Rambunctious and full of mischief, I would say he was just like me, but he was too thoughtful. Even at just five years old, he was always thinking of others. He took after his momma, and it made my heart swell. His sisters got Mary's dark hair and green eyes, but they got my fire. Stubborn, prideful, and full of spunk. I chuckled to myself, and Sierra glanced at me.

"Just thinking about the kids," I said. "They're a handful, but I wouldn't have it any other way."

She didn't say anything, but her face softened as she watched me. I wondered what she was thinking, what she saw when she looked at me. I knew she was embarrassed by her past, but I wanted to tell her it didn't matter. I intended to keep telling her that until she believed me.

Everyone had a past. I was ashamed of mine, and that was all my own doing. I doubted Sierra had a choice in anything, and I didn't want her putting any of the blame on herself. I wasn't always the best with words, and I could tell she didn't want to talk about it. Sometimes talking was necessary though. Mary taught me that.

We rounded the last bend, and the ranch came into view. The children were playing in the grass by the house. I could see Clint working on the fence for the corral. Mrs. Grady was rocking in a chair on the porch. She was the first to see us and waved.

Then the children came running. I couldn't help the giant grin at the sight of them whooping and hollering across the yard. I felt Sierra tense beside me, but she was smiling.

I hopped down from the wagon and scooped all three kids into a big hug. They all talked at once and clung to my arms and legs, and I wouldn't have it any other way. I kissed the tops of their heads and produced candy from my pocket.

Clint helped Sierra down from the wagon, and I felt a brief flare of something almost like jealousy. But of course, Clint was the perfect gentleman. His hands didn't linger on her waist, and he didn't look at her with anything more than curiosity at our new hire. I shook my head. Clint would certainly pick up on my attraction to this woman, and I knew the teasing would be endless when he did.

"Sierra, these are my children. Annie is my oldest. She's twelve. Gracie is eight, and Tuck Jr. is five." I ruffled

Junior's hair, and he pushed my hand away.

"You gonna be our momma?" Junior asked and I cringed at his question. I had spoken at length with the children about the role Sierra would play, but of course my youngest still didn't understand how it worked.

Sierra smiled at him and knelt down, so she was at his level.

"I can't replace your momma," she said. "And I don't plan to try, but I'm here to take care of you and read to you and love you like she did. Will that be alright?"

Junior nodded, then rushed forward and threw his arms around Sierra's neck. She was surprised. I saw her wince, but she didn't push the little boy away. She wrapped him in her arms. I hadn't seen his little face that content since Mary held him.

Unexpected emotion clogged my throat. I coughed to cover the feeling.

The girls hung back, watching Sierra. Annie had been resistant to this idea, but we were all saved from any awkwardness by Mrs. Grady.

"Tucker, good to see you had a safe trip to town and back," she said. She patted my cheek then turned to Sierra and grasped her hands. "And I'm so glad you're here. These children are lucky to have you. Now, I'd best be on my way."

"I'll get you back to town, Mrs. Grady," Clint rushed forward to help the older woman into the wagon.

"Oh, you boys take such good care of me," she said. "I really could drive myself to town you know, but then the scenery wouldn't be quite as nice." She winked at Sierra then and grinned cheekily at Clint.

Clint and Sierra both blushed at her words.

"I'll be back this evening," Clint said.

"You might keep your head down," I said. "Things were a little tense when we left."

Clint just laughed. "I shoulda known."

When they were out of sight, Sierra turned to me. "Will he be alright? You don't think those men…"

"He'll be fine," I assured her. "Clint's better at keeping his head down than I am."

Annie spoke up behind us. "Mrs. Grady made dinner."

I shooed the children toward the house. "You all run along inside and help Sierra get settled in. I've gotta check on the horses, and then I'll be in." Junior tucked his hand into Sierra's and led her into the house.

Most of the horses were out in the pasture, but the big stallion I had been working with was pacing in the corral. The fence looked good where Clint had patched it, but I wondered how long it would be until the big horse kicked it down again. I named him Storm, and I hadn't made much progress with him.

Yet.

I'd get through to him eventually, just like another wild spirit I knew.

I smiled at the thought of Sierra as I leaned against the fence to watch Storm. He pawed at the ground and tossed his head. He was a beautiful horse with fire in his eyes. I didn't intend to break that fire. Some men might, but not me. I wanted to teach the horse to harness it.

To work with me.

To trust me.

I chuckled to myself. The similarities really were uncanny.

"Dinner's ready." Sierra's soft voice interrupted my thoughts.

I watched her for a moment, and I could tell she was trying not to fidget under my gaze. Her hands were clasped, and her fingers twitched like she wanted to smooth her skirt or pull at her sleeve. She couldn't leave that sleeve alone ever since Harlan found the brand there. I didn't mean to stare, but I couldn't help it. I wanted to hunt down the man that did that to her and brand him.

"If you're busy or not hungry..." Sierra trailed off.

"Starving," I said. Then I smiled at her to try and ease the tension. I knew I was making her nervous with my silence, and I didn't mean to. "I don't like to miss meals with the kids. Sorry, I was just thinking. Get lost in my head sometimes."

She nodded at that and looked past me to the horse.

"He's a tricky one," I said. "Can't hardly get a hand on him, let alone a bridle or saddle."

"He's beautiful."

"Do you like horses?" I realized I knew hardly anything about this woman I was going to share my home with. I should have used the wagon ride to ask her more about herself; instead, I had brooded and worried.

"Haven't been around them much," she said. She leaned against the fence beside me, and we watched Storm nibble some grass before running the fence again. "I didn't get out much...at the saloon."

"Storm is a lot of horse, but I have a mare the kids ride. I could teach you to ride."

She nodded slowly, clearly thinking through my offer and wondering what was in it for me. "I'd like that."

"Papa!" Gracie called from the house. "Tuck's gonna eat all the biscuits!"

"Wildlings," I said. "I hope they don't scare you off."

"They're wonderful." She looked at me, and I was caught like a ship spinning in the eye of a storm. "Everything is...wonderful." She blushed then and hurried ahead of me into the house.

I had thought I was alone in my attraction, but I wondered if Sierra was hiding more than just her past. Maybe she felt the same thrill I had when I saw her at the station. Maybe she was nervous for reasons I hadn't even considered.

I wouldn't push her, but the idea of her wanting me as much as I wanted her made my heart beat in a way I thought it never would again.

Sierra

I FELL INTO my new role quickly. It had only been two days, but it felt like longer. Annie was a bit slow to accept me, but as the oldest, she had the most memories of her mother. I didn't expect her to accept me right away. I did my best to let her know I wasn't replacing anyone. The other two could hardly let go of me. They were always underfoot, hanging on my arms and asking questions. They made the days full and happy.

I was washing clothes in a bucket, with my sleeves rolled up. Tucker had taken the kids for a ride and Clint had gone off to check on the horses in the South pasture. For the first time in a long time, I was alone. Not another person in sight. I couldn't believe the freedom I felt knowing this was my life now.

The small bruises on my arms were fading into shades of green and yellow but they were still noticeable. I was always careful to keep myself covered, but with everyone away and the day being so warm, it was nice to push up my sleeves. I had finally unstrapped that blasted gun from my leg too. I managed to unbuckle the holster and bury it at the bottom of my suitcase. I was nervous with it there and wanted to ask Tucker to keep it for me, but for some reason I couldn't. I don't know if I was worried to tell him I had a pistol the whole time or worried to admit I was scared of it. I was certain he would have questions I didn't want to answer.

He never pushed, though.

The clothes were scrubbed, and my hands were like prunes. I sat back and wiped hair from my eyes. The day was warm, and washing clothes was hard work. Not that I minded. I was definitely better at washing clothes than cooking. Tucker hadn't said anything about my cooking, and I wondered if he ever would. I tried to follow the recipes and Annie helped me, but I knew it wasn't gourmet dining.

It was barely edible dining.

I blushed thinking of the previous evening's disastrous attempt at meatloaf.

Still, it meant a lot that he ate the meals without complaint.

I stood and stretched. A sudden urge to lay in the grass came over me. The sun and breeze felt nice on my bare arms, so I hiked my skirts up to my thighs and laid back. I still had hours to myself, and the laundry needed to soak. I couldn't remember the last time I took a break like this.

I closed my eyes and let the sun warm my face.

I don't know how long I laid there. I must have dozed off, but hoof-beats thrummed through the ground and woke me. I jerked upright, momentarily confused, but then I saw Tucker riding up on Max. The children weren't with him.

"Where are the children?"

He stopped near me, and I could feel the heat in his gaze. I felt the breeze on my skin and panic coursed through me. I hastily straightened my skirts, fumbling to throw them over my legs and get to my feet.

Tucker dismounted Max and was by my side in one motion. He caught my hands gently, stilling my movements.

"Who did this?" His voice was low and deadly. His eyes raked over my arms where handprint bruises were fading, but still visible.

I looked away as I repeated my question. "Where are the children?"

He was silent for a long moment and I thought he was going to press the issue, but he finally answered me.

"The children wanted to stay with Clint out on the trails a while longer. I thought I might come back and work with Storm."

I glanced at him and found his eyes still on my arms, as his thumbs smoothed small circles on the back of my hands. "I'm sorry I disturbed you. I wasn't thinking."

"Nothing to be sorry for. You can come and go as you please. I was just working on the laundry." I tried to pull away, but he didn't release me.

"Dr. Morrow will be out later today."

I tensed at his words. When I pulled away this time, he let me go. I jerked my sleeves down and turned back to the wash. I hesitated to continue with the washing because I really didn't want to soak my dress when reaching into the bucket. I tamped down my irritation.

"I don't need a doctor." I didn't care if he heard the anger in my voice. I was tired of his fussing. I didn't need his pity, but when I turned back to him, it wasn't pity I saw in his eyes, but anger. I took a step back and cursed myself for showing such weakness. I knew Tucker wouldn't hurt me, but the force of his gaze surprised me.

"What about your leg?"

"Oh, well that's my own fault," I shifted, embarrassed that he had seen my thighs. He was silent and words tumbled from my mouth. "The girls insisted I take a pistol and Charity strapped it to my leg, but I didn't know what to do with it and it chafed something awful and anyway, that's all there is to say about it."

He smiled a little at that and I couldn't help laughing at myself.

"Where is it now?"

"The pistol? I buried it at the bottom of my suitcase. I didn't know what to do with it, but I didn't want the children to find it."

"That's not a good place to keep it if you need to use it," he said.

"Didn't plan on using it. Don't know why I'd need to anyway." Clearly, I wasn't going to shoot him or his ranch hand.

He shrugged. "Lots of reasons to keep a pistol handy. Wolves, bears, mountain lions, never know when it could save your life."

"Well, it wouldn't help me anyway. I don't even know how to shoot it."

"Let's get it out of your suitcase. I can put it somewhere safe in case you change your mind." He walked toward the house, and I followed.

"It's in there." I pointed at my suitcase had wedged between my bed and the wall. He looked at me and I held my hands up. "I'm not touchin' it. I barely got the thing off my leg without losing a toe."

"Well, that would've been a shame." His eyes sparkled with amusement as he grabbed my bag from the floor.

"Damn straight. I have adorable toes." My eyes widened at my words. Where had that come from? Never in my life had I referred to my toes as adorable. But the sight of this man stretching across my bed had sent all my good sense flying out of my head.

"I'm sure they are," he murmured, and I wondered if I was supposed to hear his words. My face felt like fire and I'm sure I was blushing all the way down to my apparently adorable toes.

"A Deringer." Tucker pulled the little pistol from its holster and turned it over in his hands. I froze.

I was back in the room when I was fifteen. My wrist still burning from the brand Jackson had put there. The iron shoved back in the potbelly stove in the corner of his room. "Behave," he'd said, "or you'll get another brand." I didn't know of any girls with more than one brand, but I imagined he would put it somewhere only he could see. Jackson wanted me, but someone was paying him a lot of money to have me first. That didn't stop him from having a little fun with me. It was only fun for him. And when I told him I'd kill him, he'd pulled out his pistol.

"I don't care how much money Preston McKlellan is paying to have you, you ever threaten me again, girl, and you won't like where I shove this pistol. Get me?" I understood perfectly, and I never forgot that pistol. The pistol that Tucker held in his hands. I didn't look at it closely before, but Charity must have stolen it from Jackson. She was the only one that could have gotten close enough. The only one that was trusted in his rooms alone.

Oh, Charity, what did you do?

Tucker

SIERRA WENT rigid. Her breath came in short gasps and her eyes stared unseeing, at the pistol in my hands. I slipped it back in the holster and set it out of sight.

"Sierra?" I moved toward her slowly, my hands raised, hoping she saw the gun was gone.

She jerked at my touch, but her eyes focused on my face.

"You with me?" I spoke quietly, my words barely more than a whisper. I reached up to cup her face and she surprised me by leaning into my touch. She closed her eyes. A single tear slipped down her cheek. I brushed it away with my thumb.

"I'm sorry." Her voice was hoarse with unshed tears. "I don't know what came over me. I...that pistol...I didn't look at it when Charity gave it to me. I didn't realize it was Jackson's. Charity must have taken it from him." She pulled away from me and wrapped her arms tightly around herself. I wanted to follow her retreat and gather her in my arms. I hated that she felt she needed to hide from me. From anyone.

"And you're worried for her?" Her body was tense, her eyes darting toward the door as if she might run back to her old life given the chance. But it wasn't her old life she wanted, just her friend. I could tell Sierra was scared for Charity.

Sierra nodded. "Charity is Jackson's favorite. He trusts her. I don't know what he'll do if he finds out she stole from him." Her voice cracked and a sob escaped.

I reached for her even though I shouldn't. She surprised me again by leaning against my chest. Her head tucked under my chin, and my arms wrapped around her small body. She was warm and soft against me and despite her distress, I couldn't help enjoying how nice it was. But she didn't need that from me now. She needed comfort, and that's all this was.

"Your friend sounds like a smart girl. I'm sure she knew what she was doing." I didn't know her friend, but I had to hope my words weren't just false assurances. Sierra was worried for her friend, and she didn't need anything else to worry about. She needed to believe Charity knew what she was doing when she took the gun. "She got you out. That couldn't have been easy. If she could slip you out under Jackson's nose, a little pistol wouldn't be anything to worry about."

Sierra nodded against me. After a moment, she pulled away. She wiped at her face and smoothed her dress. "I need to finish the laundry. The children will be back soon, and I haven't even started dinner."

"Don't worry about dinner. I told them we'd cook over a campfire tonight. They like to pretend they're traveling on the Oregon trail after a day of riding." I shrugged. I wouldn't mind a little campfire cooking too. Sierra's cooking was fine, and I'd never criticize, but I could tell it was new to her. I figured we would all enjoy a break from a normal dinner.

"That sounds nice." I thought she might say something more, but she turned quickly and left. I heard the door shut behind her as she went back to the washing.

The pistol lay where I left it. Guns were tools to me. I didn't know why Sierra reacted that way when she saw this pistol in particular, but I reckoned there was more to it than just concern over her friend.

I needed to shoot something.

I hadn't been out to the range in a while, and I

was itching for a reason to blow some holes in something. Between the men in town and whoever hurt Sierra, I had plenty of motivation for some sharp shooting.

I grabbed my six-shooters and headed outside. I mounted Max quickly then urged him into a gallop and leaned low over his neck. My shooting range wasn't just some targets set against the mountain. It was a course that required focus, skill, and intensity. A little anger didn't hurt anything either.

In fact, I was at my best when I was angry.

Max knew where to go. He galloped through the valley and into the narrow gully where the rocks pressed in on either side. I ducked under branches and leaned away from rocky outcroppings. I gripped Max with my legs and held the reins in my teeth. Then I drew both pistols and started shooting.

Overhead, the dummies stuffed with twigs and straw leaned precariously from their hiding places. Clint set up my course, and he had been busy. I almost didn't see the first one, but my aim was true, and then I was in my element. Shooting from either hand, I took down the dummies in one pass.

Twelve dummies.

Twelve shots.

I eased Max into a trot and then a walk. We circled back around through the valley and came up just below the house. I reloaded my pistols and dismounted. I had a small target set about a hundred yards out and took some shots at it to cool down.

The anger still simmered, but it didn't course through me like hot lava. I could think more clearly now, and I knew Sierra didn't need my anger. I didn't know what she needed from me except respect and a place she could feel safe. I might hope for more. A lot more, but I wasn't going to push her. She didn't need that from me right now.

She had leaned into my embrace, but she was upset. I couldn't let myself think there was more to it than a woman needing a friend to lean on. A friend. That's what I could be, even if the mere thought of Sierra sent blood rushing south.

I shifted my stance to ease the growing discomfort in my pants and popped off another shot at the target.

Max nickered and tossed his head toward the house. I followed his gaze and was surprised to see Sierra watching me from the back door. She leaned against the door frame. Even at this distance, I could see her perfect curves. The breeze lifted the ends of her long hair, and a few strands blew across her face. She watched me for a moment longer, then turned her back and went into the house.

I holstered my guns and hiked up the hill with Max in tow. Sierra hadn't looked upset, but I felt the need to check on her even though she didn't seem to appreciate my attentions most of the time. Still, I couldn't stop thinking about the way she felt in my arms.

I didn't want her to be upset, but I wouldn't object if she needed to be held.

Shit. I was in over my head already. I should have just put it out of my mind. A man like me was the last thing Sierra needed. She didn't need a hotheaded, washed-up old gunslinger.

She was by the window when I walked in. The late afternoon sun cast a warm glow across her features. When she looked at me, it was more than just the setting sun reflected in her eyes. I was surprised by the fire I saw — a spark I knew was inside her but had rarely seen. There was a new determination about her, and I didn't know where it had come from, but I liked it.

I liked her.

I smiled and I'm sure I looked goofy as a schoolboy, but if it made her smile back like that, I would do it every day.

She didn't need me, but I damn sure needed her.

Sierra

TUCKER WAS a dangerous man. I'd known that from the first moment I saw him at the train station. He was dangerous, but he was good too. I watched him with the horses, with his kids and Clint, and he was always gentle, always patient. I hadn't known a man like that before.

Then I saw him with the pistol — Jackson's pistol — and then later with his own. He shot that man in town, but I didn't really think about the actual shooting. Just that it had happened.

Tucker was a man who knew how to handle a gun.

A few days ago, that thought might have scared me. If I had known I was coming to live with a man who carried a pistol like an extension of his arm, I never would have left my room at the saloon. But now, seeing him in person, I wasn't scared.

I was excited.

Thrilled.

For some reason, the sight of Tucker firing his pistols with such intensity and precision awakened my spirit. This man would protect me. He already had, but seeing him like that, and letting him hold me, it let the hope that had been growing in my chest finally bloom.

"I want to learn to shoot," I said.

I could tell those were not the words he expected when he came into the house. He was probably worried that his shooting had frightened me. I couldn't blame him, considering what a mess I looked earlier when I saw Jackson's gun. But the shock of that had worn off — the shock of everything had finally worn off — and I felt a fierceness in my spirit I had never felt in my whole life.

I had let Jackson and Preston beat me down and nearly put out my fire, but not anymore.

"Will you teach me?" Now the nerves hit me. Tucker was still standing there, staring at me like I had sprouted another head. I realized I already assumed he would say yes, but now that I asked, he might say no. I resisted the urge to shrink away from my question, to wring my hands or back down. If he wouldn't teach me then I would teach myself.

But I really hoped he would teach me.

"You want to learn to shoot?" He repeated my question back to me. His brow furrowed in confusion, but his eyes sparkled with interest.

I nodded, not trusting myself to speak again until he answered.

"Alright," he smiled at me. "Might as well start now."

"Now?" I squeaked.

He shrugged. "Don't know what else to do until the kids get back."

I could think of a few things we could do.

No. I wasn't going there. Tucker was nothing but polite and professional toward me and, besides, I had sworn off men forever. I wouldn't take his kindness for granted or mistake it for interest in something more.

"I have a target we can set up in front of the house." Tucker went out the front door and I followed.

He set everything up and handed me one of his pistols. It was much larger and heavier than Jackson's pistol; I could barely fit my hand around the hilt. I clutched it with both hands. Tucker cupped my hands with one of his and showed me the parts of the gun.

His voice was steady and soft. He made the gun seem like a tool more than something deadly. I guess it was both, really.

"Ready to try shooting at the target?" he asked.

"I can barely lift it." I angled my body toward the target, but I couldn't hold the gun steady. I could only lift it to about waist high, and the barrel pointed to the ground. My hands ached and my arms shook.

"Here." Tucker stepped behind me and I could feel the heat of him through my cotton dress. Then he was pressed against me as one hand wrapped around both of mine and helped steady the gun. His other hand rested on my waist. He nudged my feet with his foot, adjusting my stance. "That's better."

His breath was warm against my ear as he leaned in to help me line up with the target. I held my breath.

"Easy now, pull the trigger nice and slow. It'll kick a bit, but I got you," he said. Then his hand squeezed my waist gently. "And don't forget to breathe."

With an exhale, I pulled the trigger and the gun rocked in my hands. The report of the shot echoed through the valley and made my head ring. I breathed heavily. Tucker steadied the gun, and me. I was shaking. I didn't even know if we hit the target.

"It's a lot of gun to start with," he said. "We can try with the rifle tomorrow. Clint has it with him now. I don't have anything else, except..."

"Jackson's gun."

Tucker nodded. "It would be a better pistol to start with, but we can keep using this one too."

I let out a shaky breath, but I was determined to do this. I needed to do this.

"Let's try with the other pistol," I said. "What kind is it?" I didn't want to keep calling it 'Jackson's gun'.

"A Deringer," he said. He didn't say anything more as he went to retrieve the pistol, but something shone on his face that made me think he was proud of me. Maybe even impressed.

The smaller pistol fit in my hand much better. It was lighter too, and I didn't have any trouble holding it out in front of me. My hands shook only a little. Tucker still stood close to me, his hand hovering but not touching. I set my jaw and gripped the pistol tighter, willing my hands to be steady.

"Whenever you're ready, just squeeze the trigger. Brace yourself, but this one won't kick as much." Tucker moved his hand away from mine but didn't step back. I appreciated his solid form behind me for more than one reason. I pulled the trigger and the little gun jumped in my hands. Tucker's hands caught mine before I dropped it.

"Did I hit it?" I squinted at the target but couldn't see any sign of a bullet hole.

"Grazed it, I reckon," Tucker said. "You did good."

"Are you just saying that to make me feel better?" I narrowed my eyes at him.

He laughed and held up his hands, "I never lie. You did good for someone who's never held a gun before."

"I've held one, just never fired it." I instantly regretted my words as memories of Preston surfaced. Apparently, I always ended up around men who had a thing for guns. I shook my head, disgusted with myself for even thinking of Tucker in the same instance I thought of Jackson and Preston.

Tucker was nothing like them.

"That's probably enough practice for today." He gently took the gun from my hands.

"I only fired two shots." I put my hands on my hips in the universal stance of a woman ready to argue.

"It's enough for today," he shrugged. "Gotta keep you wantin' more." He grinned a little and I wondered if he intended for his words to send shivers all through me. I was sure he didn't. I glared at his retreating form.

"I should at least shoot 'til I hit the target."

"You did. I said you grazed it." His lips were still curled into a frustrating and distracting smirk. He looked good when he teased me. I stopped that thought before it could form. I was not going to think about how kissable his lips were. I had never kissed a man, not really. Preston smashed his lips to mine on occasion, but I wouldn't call that kissing. Not the kind of kissing I would do with Tucker. No, I wouldn't think about kissing him.

"You're thinking about something awful hard," Tucker said. His eyes searched mine as if he could hear my thoughts. I was glad he couldn't. I felt myself blush and opened my mouth to tell him I was thinking of absolutely nothing when the sound of a horse and wagon drew our attention to the road.

I unconsciously stepped back as Tucker stepped forward. I didn't like how quickly my boldness could leave me. I still jumped at every sound and wanted to hide the moment I heard the wagon approaching. The kids and Clint were all out on horses and our wagon was in the shed. Tucker didn't seem worried, but I couldn't help but think of the men in town, or Preston finally coming to drag me back.

"I'm sure it's just the doctor," Tucker said. "Clint should be back with the kids soon, too. Junior needs to get his stitches out."

"Of course." I let out a breath and it came out as nervous laughter. I was smoothing my skirt again and I forced my hands to be still.

"You don't have to talk with her, but I'd like you to meet her," he said softly. "But you don't have to."

I didn't need a doctor. I wanted to put my foot down on the subject again, but Tucker wasn't forcing anything on me. He was being reasonable, and he was right. There was no reason I couldn't at least meet the doctor. If I was going to work for him, and I fully intended to stay here as long as the children needed me, it would be good to meet new people.

"I would like to meet her," I said. "I'll say hello,

but that's it." I started to tell him not to mention anything to her, but my eyes must have said it because he held his hands up in surrender.

"I'll just introduce you and won't say another word." He crossed his heart as if to prove the truth of his words.

The horse and wagon crested the hill and came across the yard. The doctor reigned in the horse and Tucker went to help her down from the wagon.

She was younger than I expected with fiery red hair that was pulled back in a long braid. Some of her hair had come loose and framed her face in soft curls. She was taller than me and seemed stronger too. Like she never took shit from a man in her life. For some reason I wanted the ground to open up and swallow me whole. I felt out of place next to this woman that was a doctor and could drive a horse and wagon across the countryside on her own.

This was the woman Tucker needed in his life, not me.

Tucker frowned at me, his eyes full of concern, and I tried to smooth my features. I tried not to let my discomfort show. I tried to hide the sudden and oppressing sense of inadequacy I felt.

Tucker introduced me. "Dr. Morrow, this is Sierra. She arrived recently to help with the children and keep me in line."

"You certainly need it." The doctor laughed, then she held her hand out to me. "Please, call me Caroline."

"It's nice to meet you." I grasped her hand cautiously and she nearly took my arm off with her firm shake.

"Sorry, I'm so used to these men." She jabbed her thumb in Tucker's direction. "I forget not everyone is going to try and crush my hand in their grip."

"I've never tried to crush your hand," Tucker grumbled.

"Not intentionally." She smiled, then turned to me. "'Course he's about the only one in town that will shake my hand."

"Why's that?" I asked.

"A lot of men in town aren't crazy about the idea of a female doctor," she said. "I've gotten used to it." I could tell she hadn't. Not entirely, anyway.

"The kids aren't back yet, but I'll ride out and get them," Tucker said. He grabbed Max and headed out before I could give him a look that said, 'I know what you're doing.'

"I needed a break anyway," Caroline said. "You wouldn't believe the day I've had." She laughed again as she sank down in a chair on the porch.

"Would you like something to drink?"

Caroline waved her hand to the chair beside her. "No, don't fuss over me. Just sit down and relax. I bet you've had a long day too, with the kids to look after and the menfolk. They need more taking care of than the kids."

I sat in the chair next to her but perched on the edge, not sure what to do with myself. I didn't spend a lot of time relaxing with the other girls in Jackson's saloon. I considered Charity and Maggie my friends, but I didn't think the conversations we usually had were things normal women talked about. I'm sure Caroline didn't gossip about men's dicks, but then again, she was a doctor, so maybe so.

Caroline chatted easily about her day, and I found myself relaxing as she talked. She was animated and used her whole body to tell the stories. I was surprised to discover that I liked her. I actually liked listening to her talk and laughing at her stories even if I didn't know any of the people she was telling me about. She ended her story, and we were quiet for a while, just watching the horses in the field.

"I heard about what happened in town."

My body went stiff at her words.

"Those idiots. They took Bomey to the barbershop and he nearly lost his leg, which he would have deserved." She sighed. "Sometimes, I wish I wasn't the only doctor in town."

I didn't want to talk about that day or anything else to do with me, but I was curious now about what happened to the man Tucker had shot.

"Did you treat him?"

"They finally brought him to me when he was about half dead," she said. "I worked on him all night, but he'll live and keep his leg too."

I nodded because it seemed like the thing to do, not because I cared that the man would live. I only wished Tucker had shot Harlan instead.

"I hope you don't judge us because of those goons," Caroline said. "Most people in town are really nice, and honestly, there aren't even that many men that give me crap anymore. Just like anywhere, I suppose, they're cautious of outsiders. Once they warm up to you, then you're practically family."

Her words surprised me, and it must have shown on my face.

"I wouldn't just say that. They really are nice when you get to know them."

"It's not that, I just…it doesn't matter. I'll keep that in mind." I didn't want to go to town in the near future, or ever, but I kept that thought to myself. I didn't know why she worried about me judging the town. What did anyone care about my opinion? No one ever cared before, but I had a new life now and for some reason I kept thinking the old rules applied. They didn't.

That also meant it might be alright to talk to this doctor. I wouldn't even know how or where to start. I really didn't need medical attention. I figured if anything was seriously wrong with me, I would have known by now. But it would be nice to talk to someone.

Maybe.

I chewed my lip and worried my hands.

"I'm sorry. I shouldn't have even brought it up," Caroline said. "I just know what it's like to be a new woman in this town and I wanted you to know it gets better. Despite what some may say, this town is lucky to have Tucker West. Clint is a good man too, and we're lucky to have a quality sheriff. Tuff is a straight shooter. Not many towns are that lucky."

"It's fine. I understand, and thank you." I did appreciate Caroline being honest with me. "I was just thinking...Tucker wanted me to talk with you, and I'm fine really, there's no reason to talk. But it is nice to have another woman to confide in."

Caroline nodded, her face open and listening. She didn't say anything, and part of me hoped Tucker and the kids would come riding into the yard and interrupt this moment. Another part of me hoped they wouldn't. Maybe Tucker was right, and it would do me some good to talk. It was certainly easier to think about talking with Caroline than anyone else. The idea of Tucker knowing anything more than he already did made me nearly turn inside out. I already felt like the man could read my soul. I didn't need him to *actually* know all my secrets.

"You know what happened in town," I started.
If she knew about that then she probably already knew
about my brand. I imagined this town was full of gossips
like any other. "Then you probably heard about my...you
know..." For some reason I couldn't say it. I didn't want
to acknowledge the mark upon my skin.

"You can tell me anything you want. I'll listen
whenever you're ready." Caroline put her hand on my
arm. "The town hasn't been gossiping like you think. I
heard most of what happened from Harlan and his men
when they came to my clinic, and I take most of what they
say with a grain of salt."

I nodded at her words. I wasn't sure if it was true
about the lack of gossip or if she said it just to make me
feel better, but I appreciated it either way. Whatever she
heard, she was willing to listen to me. Maybe even willing
to be my first friend in this town.

Female friend anyway. I liked to think Tucker was
my friend.

"I'm sure you heard about the...mark on my wrist.
I was a working girl in Missouri, but I wanted a new life."
Once I got started, the words came easy. I didn't know
Caroline's past. I didn't know if she really understood the
weight of everything I was sharing, but she was easy to
talk to.

She didn't push, and she didn't switch into doctor
mode either, even though I could tell she was concerned at

times. She just…listened. And she was angry, too. I could tell she tried to hold it in, but even that made me feel better. I didn't realize how much I wanted someone to be angry with me. Then I thought of Tucker's anger at the men in town. His anger when he saw the bruises on my arms. Everyone tried to hide their anger, maybe thinking it was to protect me. That I couldn't handle it. But I realized anger was exactly what I needed.

I just hoped it didn't swallow me up.

Tucker

I T WAS NEARLY dark by the time I rounded up the kids and Clint and got back to the house. Sierra was probably cursing my name over the fact that I left her with the doctor. I was surprised to find the two of them laughing and chatting like old friends when I returned.

Caroline was a good doctor, and I was glad Sierra had taken to her. Caroline needed a friend as much as Sierra needed one.

It was great to see both of them relaxed and

laughing, though I would be lying if I said Sierra's laugh didn't make my heart beat faster. I could watch that woman smile all day.

"Ladies." I tipped my hat to them, and they both rolled their eyes. "Sorry to keep you waiting, Doc. The kids get carried away on the trails sometimes. You're welcome to stay the night."

"No, I can make it over to Mrs. Anderson's place before it gets too dark. Let me take a look at Junior and get those stitches out." Caroline waved me off as she jumped to her feet.

"I'll go with you." Clint leaned against the railing of the porch. "I don't mind riding in the dark. Just gotta watch out for the ghosts."

"Oh, you two." Caroline laughed. "What in the world would a girl do without you mother hens?"

"Reckon the ghosts would get you," Clint said seriously.

I chuckled. Clint was only half joking about ghosts. He was convinced the woods north of the house were haunted. We were also in agreement that Caroline wouldn't ride out on her own if we could help it. During the day was one thing, but you never knew what was prowling around after dark, and the good doctor's sense of self-preservation left something to be desired.

"I'll get the campfire going." I called for Gracie

and Annie to help me as Caroline corralled Junior.

I was hoping for a moment to talk with Caroline before she left. Not that I wanted Sierra thinking I was talking about her. I was just worried. And while I didn't expect or want Caroline to break Sierra's confidence, I trusted that she would tell me if Sierra was okay or not.

When the campfire was roaring, I sent the girls in to help Sierra gather supplies. Caroline had finished up with Tuck Jr. and was packing her bag in her wagon.

"Well, your little man healed up nicely," she said. "I don't think he'll even have a scar."

"Reckon he wouldn't have minded a little scar to show how tough he is." That kid was a wrecking ball of energy and had more visits with Caroline than any kid in town.

She laughed, and silence fell between us as I tried to think of a way to ask about Sierra. I didn't want to seem like I was prying, but that's exactly what I was doing. Lucky for me, the doctor was a smart woman, and she knew where my mind was headed.

"She's okay," Caroline said softly. "At least, she will be."

I nodded. "But she's not okay right now."

"She's been through a lot, Tucker." Caroline looked away from me and her eyes glistened in the low light. She blinked and wiped at her face. "She's strong, though.

Stronger than a lot of women…a lot of people… I've met. I like her, and I'm glad you hired her. Though I could cut the tension between the two of you with a scalpel."

I whipped my head around at her words.

She laughed. "Oh come on, it's obvious you're attracted to her."

"She doesn't need that right now," I said. My voice was rougher than I intended, but Caroline didn't back down.

"You might be exactly what she needs."

"I doubt she's interested in a man like me. She needs someone better than me." I wanted Caroline's words to be true, but I couldn't accept that I was the best man for Sierra.

I was too rough, too angry, too quick to draw my gun.

"Why don't you let her decide?" Caroline shrugged. "She likes you."

I felt numb as I helped Caroline into her wagon. The doctor wouldn't lie to me, but surely she was wrong. I was certain the attraction was one-sided. There was no way Sierra would go for a man like me, but now that the thought was in my head, it wouldn't leave.

Sierra liked me.

"Ready to go, Doc?" Clint trotted over on his horse, Colonel. The flashy paint horse was a stout, sturdy horse, and sure-footed. "Sierra packed some food for you."

"Thank you!" Caroline shouted toward the porch where Sierra was watching the kids by the campfire.

Sierra waved. Her whole body was more relaxed than I had ever seen her. She caught my eye, and I wondered if she blushed or if it was just the firelight dancing over her face.

"Thanks for coming out, Doc." I shook her hand and then patted her horse on the neck.

"Anytime, Tucker. You know I like visiting, and now that Sierra's here, I have even more reason to make the trip. It's nice to have a new friend."

"Let's go before the ghosts start movin'," Clint said.

I shook my head as Caroline laughed and snapped the reins. Her wagon took off with a creak and bumped across the yard out of sight.

I joined the kids by the campfire and checked on the beans in the cast iron pot. The kids were throwing sticks into the flames and playing a silly game. They seemed happier since Sierra joined us. I knew Annie was taking some time to warm up to the idea of Sierra, but I even caught her leaning in for a hug and following in Sierra's footsteps when she was hanging the wash or working in the garden.

A rustle of fabric from the porch caught my attention, and Sierra was already by my side when I turned toward the sound.

"Will Clint be alright in the dark?" she asked.

I nodded. "Clint's tougher than a cougar and twice as quick."

She laughed at that, but I could tell she still worried. She chewed her lower lip and hugged herself.

"It's not far to Mrs. Anderson's place, and she'll be glad of Caroline's company for the night," I said. "And if the ghosts spook Clint on the way, he'll sleep in the barn and come back in the morning."

"Is he serious about the ghosts?" Sierra looked at me with narrowed eyes, and I could tell she thought one or both of us was pulling her leg.

"Only partly." I threw a stick into the fire and the sparks crackled into the dark sky. "Clint can be a little jumpy. One night, he was riding north of the farm, and he swears he saw something in the trees. I reckon it was an albino deer or something, but he says it was a woman. I think he had a bit too much to drink and was feeling a bit lonely. Anyway, next thing I know, he's found an old graveyard out a ways to the north, and now he's convinced the woods are haunted."

"He doesn't seem like the type to believe in ghosts." Sierra's eyes looked to the north of the property where the shadow of the tree line was barely visible in the fading light.

"When you've done the work we've done, it's easy to believe in them," I said. "Especially when you have so many ghosts of your own."

I felt her eyes on me as I stared into the flames. She placed her hand on my arm and moved closer. I turned when I felt the heat of her, and it felt warmer to me than the roaring fire. Her head tilted up and I was surprised by how close I was to her. How close her lips were to mine. I wanted to lean down and close the distance between us, but I had only just come to the idea of Sierra maybe liking me, and I wasn't going to make the first move tonight. When she was ready for that, I was more than willing though.

"Thank you." Her voice was barely more than a whisper. I felt her breath more than heard her words.

"For what?" I was thinking about kissing her and couldn't process what she might be thanking me for.

"Everything." She motioned toward the campfire, the kids, and then between us. "This. And thank you for making me meet Caroline. It's nice to have a friend."

"She said the same thing." I thought Sierra should know it wasn't one-sided. I was right in thinking the doctor needed a friend, too.

Sierra seemed surprised at my words, but then she nodded, a smile on her face.

Tuck Junior ran over then and grabbed us both in a hug. Then Gracie joined in. Annie hung back, but I could tell she was wondering if she was too old for group hugs.

"Come on, Sparky." I hadn't used my nickname for her in forever. I wondered when I stopped. Her face lit up, and she barreled into us. I wrapped the kids in one arm and the other around Sierra.

She didn't object. In fact, she leaned in so her head was tucked against my chest.

I hoped for more with Sierra, but if this was all I ever got, it would be enough.

Sierra

I LAID AWAKE in my small room staring at the ceiling long after the kids went to bed and the campfire died down. I couldn't stop thinking about everything that happened. It seemed surreal to think of everything I did in a single day.

Fired a pistol — *two* pistols.

Made a new friend.

Talked about my past.

And then there was the campfire. It wasn't just the time spent by the fire that was nice, but Tucker being so close. Leaning my head against his chest and feeling his arms around me. I couldn't get it out of my mind. I couldn't stop thinking about the way he felt. How strong and hard he was, and yet, how perfectly we melded together by the firelight.

How perfectly I fit against him.

I sighed and stared at the ceiling some more. I willed sleep to come, but then I heard something outside. I laid still and strained to hear what it was. A horse nickered. I heard Tucker's bedroom door open and then the front door. Low voices outside.

I relaxed back into my bed. Clint was probably just getting back.

The front door opened and closed, then I heard Tucker's bedroom door close quietly. I sighed and rolled on my side, staring at my closed door, and thinking of Tucker's door across the house. I wondered if he had been lying awake, too.

I wondered if we were staring at each other and didn't even know it.

I woke with the sunrise and was already making biscuits when Tucker came out of his room. I watched him as he leaned over to pull his boots on. I nearly dropped my bowl when he caught me looking. I felt myself turn red, so I busied myself with the dough to hide my face.

Tucker's boots fell heavy across the floor, and then he was behind me, looking over my shoulder to see what I was doing.

"Good morning," he said. His breath warmed my neck. "Making biscuits?"

I nodded dumbly, not trusting my voice.

"Kids still sleeping?" I felt him look toward the loft.

I nodded again, as I kneaded the dough with more force than was necessary.

"Easy." His hands covered mine. I resisted the urge to lean back into him. "What did the biscuits ever do to you?" He chuckled against my neck and then stepped away. I sagged at the loss of his heat. Even though we had barely been touching, it was like the warmth of him held me up, and now I felt the chill in the room I hadn't noticed before.

"Did Clint make it home okay?" I needed something else to focus on, and Clint seemed a safe topic.

"Yeah, some limbs were down across the road to Mrs. Anderson's, so it's a good thing he went along with Caroline. It delayed him some in getting back, but I reckon he's already up and working with Storm. No rest for the weary or the wicked." He grinned and winked at me, then ducked out the front door.

I formed the biscuits and put them in the potbellied stove. Wiping my hands on my apron, I watched Tucker and Clint out the front window. Clint was in with Storm, and Tucker leaned against the fence. They both had such patience with that horse. I could tell the big stallion had calmed just in the short time I had been here. He spent most of his time grazing now instead of pacing the fence, and he wasn't as quick to rear up or try to kick the men.

I liked watching Tucker work with the horses. He was gentle with them and always knew just what to do. The horses trusted him.

It's how he was with his kids too.

And me.

Not that I thought he was treating me like a skittish horse…but maybe he was. I shook my head at the thought. It was just his way. He knew what animals…and people… needed. Sure, I saw another part of him in town when he was dealing with Harlan and his men, but it didn't scare me.

Until I met Tucker, I never dreamed a man could be both good and bad. It made my heart race and heat pool in my belly when I thought of the way he protected me, cared for me. He was like two sides of a coin. Each side was unique, but they were both part of the same coin.

I wanted all of him.

And ever since yesterday, after my talk with Caroline and then spending time with him by the campfire, I had started to think he might want me too. And not just in the way a man wants a woman. Though I had to admit I wanted him in that way, too.

I blushed at the thought and turned away from the window.

The kids stirred upstairs, and I busied myself making gravy and setting the table to keep my mind off Tucker West and how good he looked in a pair of jeans.

After breakfast, Clint drove the kids into town for school. They didn't go every day, but they went when the school was open.

The wagon disappeared down the road and all I could think about was having a whole day alone with Tucker. I pushed the thought out of my mind. We both had things to do. He had horses to tend, and I had a house to clean. With the kids gone for the day, I could get a lot done. They were helpful but always underfoot, and they seemed to perpetually shed dirt, grass, and leaves in the house.

"What are you thinking about?" Tucker stood with his arms crossed, leaning back against the front porch post.

I realized I was smiling to myself, and I was glad it was just thoughts of the children that had me smiling and not the things I wanted to do with Tucker West.

"Just thinking about how much more cleaning I can get done without Tuck Junior's help." I laughed.

He chuckled. "How about we do something fun first?"

My heart stopped. Here he was, looking handsome as sin and talking about doing something fun. I might have imagined doing things with him, but now that he was possibly insinuating something, my courage left me. My mouth was dry, and I must have looked something close to panicked because he was beside me in two steps. Holding my arms.

"There's a waterfall in the mountains," he said. He didn't even mention my reaction; he just held me and talked. "It'll get too cold soon and we won't be able to see it, but the weather is perfect today and I thought you might like to go for a ride. On a horse."

I laughed nervously at the fact he felt the need to clarify we would be riding a horse. Had my face been that transparent? I blushed to think he might have known where my mind went. It seemed like all I did was blush around this man.

"I'd love that," I said, and I was surprised my voice sounded normal.

"Great." He smiled. "I'll grab the horse."

Wait. Horse. Not horses?

If this man expected me to ride on a horse with him, well...I would gladly ride on a horse with him.

Tucker returned with Max, and I was surprised he didn't have a saddle on him.

"It's not a bad ride up to the waterfall, but it's easier with one horse and it's more comfortable riding double without the saddle," he explained. "But if you want your own horse, I can get Colonel." Tucker seemed a bit shy and unsure of himself all of a sudden.

"It's fine." I smiled and reached out for his arm to reassure him. "I was just surprised, but this is…perfect."

Tucker mounted Max in one motion and then reached down to pull me up behind him.

"Hold on," he said.

I pressed myself against his back and wrapped my arms around his waist. Tucker covered my hands with one of his and urged Max into a trot. I didn't know if I really needed to hold on so tightly, but I wanted to, and I think Tucker liked the closeness, too. I rested my cheek against his back and breathed in the mountain air.

I didn't care if we ever reached the waterfall. I could spend the rest of the day…the rest of my life… riding a horse with Tucker West.

Tucker

THE WATERFALL was more beautiful than I remembered, but it could have been the look on Sierra's face that made it feel that way. I staked out Max along the river so he could graze and reach the water. Then I led Sierra closer to the waterfall.

It wasn't the biggest fall in the area, but in my opinion, it was the most stunning. The rocks sparkled in the morning sun, as water cascaded over smoky quartz and blue beryl crystals. I didn't tell many people about this waterfall because I knew some would be wanting to try and mine the area, and even though it was on my property, that didn't always keep out people hoping to find their fortune in the hills.

"It's beautiful," Sierra whispered. Her eyes sparkled brighter than the crystals as she watched the water cascade down the mountain.

"Come on. I usually find a few good crystals below the falls." I held her hand and led her closer to the water.

Beneath the falls, the water was still. The pool was nearly black from the depth, and as the water flowed farther down the mountain, it meandered in a gentle path. Smooth stones lined the riverbed. The sunlight sparkled where it caught the edges of crystals hidden beneath the surface.

I led Sierra to a section of wide, shallow water and kicked off my boots. I pulled off my socks and rolled up my pant legs.

She blushed and looked away.

"The water's nice here. Not as cold as it looks." I pointed back toward the waterfall where I knew caves dotted the mountain side. "There are some hot springs back in there that feed this pool. This close to the falls, it still feels pretty warm."

"Hot springs?" Sierra squinted at the falls as if she could see past the water and into the caves beyond. "I knew a girl from Arkansas that talked about hot springs. I always thought that sounded nice." She sighed.

"I can take you to the hot springs too, another time, if you'd like." I held her hand and pulled her close to me.

She nodded, her wide eyes looking between our hands and my face.

"'Course, we'd take off more than just our shoes at the hot springs," I said.

Sierra blushed and looked away, but I could see a small smile tugging at the corner of her mouth.

I let go of her and waded out into the water.

I wiggled my toes into the rocks. They were mostly smooth under my feet, and I felt for the rough edges typical of crystals. Sierra sat on the grass and watched me.

"You comin' in?" I splashed water in her direction, and she squealed even though it didn't touch her. I reached down and fished a crystal out of the rocks. It was about the size of my thumb and blue like the sky before a storm. I sloshed out of the water and plopped down beside Sierra. I held out my hand to her and she gasped at the crystal I held.

"You just found this?" She took it from me and turned it over in her hands.

I nodded. "You can find some too if you come with me."

"I can find some from here." She craned her neck to peer into the clear water as if to prove her point.

I chuckled and got back to my feet, brushing grass

from my clothes. "Suit yourself, but I think your toes —
your *adorable* toes — would enjoy this." I turned away
but could feel the blush radiating from her face. I laughed
to myself as she muttered something under her breath.

I heard a rustling of fabric and turned to see Sierra
standing closer to the water. She walked along the shore
until she reached a large flat stone protruding above the
waterline. I saw her intention as she gathered up her skirts
and prepared to leap the short distance to the stone.

Even from where I stood, I could tell the stone was
covered in a fine layer of moss.

Slippery moss.

I opened my mouth to call out a warning, but
Sierra leapt forward at that moment. One foot, then the
other landed on the rock, and slipped off just as quick.

I splashed toward her as her feet went out from
under her and she fell backward into the shallow water.

She spluttered and gasped as I scooped her up.

"Easy, I've got you." My eyes scanned her, searching
for any sign of injury. "Are you alright? Anything hurt?"

"Just my pride." She huffed out a laugh and pushed
wet strands of hair away from her face.

Knowing she wasn't hurt, I let out a chuckle.

She weighed hardly anything in my arms, even with
her skirts sopping wet. I could feel the heat of her through
her cold clothes, and even as the dampness seeped into my
own clothing, I felt my skin heat up.

I could feel the heat of my own gaze and she gasped when she met my eyes.

Her tongue darted out nervously to run along her lower lip, and it nearly made me come undone.

"Come on, let's get you back on dry land," I said gruffly. The tightness in my pants would have us both feeling uncomfortable if I didn't put some distance between us soon. The last thing I wanted to do was make Sierra uncomfortable.

"It's alright, you can put me down." She wiggled in my arms and I lost my footing as I stepped from the shifting stones of the creek bed to the dry sandy shore.

"Oh!" she exclaimed as we both fell forward.

I braced myself to keep from falling on her and she ended up beneath me.

Her breath was warm on my face, and I could feel her breasts against my chest as she took in short breaths. She closed her eyes and placed a hand on my chest.

"Sierra." I said her name, and her eyes flashed to my face. I should have let her go then. Kissed her forehead and shown her some pretty rocks in the river. But I liked the way she felt against me. And with the way she looked at me, I knew she liked it too.

"Tucker." She said it in a breathy way that had me thinking about all the other ways I wanted her to say my name.

It took all my control not to take her right there on

the smooth sand by the crystal river, even though I could tell she was thinking the same thing. This woman wanted me, and I wanted her, but I didn't want to mess it up. I didn't want to push before she was ready.

Still, her mouth was soft and open, and I was drawn to it like a moth to a flame. I closed the gap between us, but paused just before our lips met.

"Is this alright?" I didn't want there to be any confusion or misunderstanding between us. The situation had escalated far more than I expected when I'd offered to show her the waterfall. I didn't bring her up here to ravish her, and I wanted to make sure she knew that.

She nodded and I felt the movement of her lips as she breathed out her answer.

"Yes."

I descended on her like a drowning man seeking air. Her lips were like rose petals. She melted into me and her small hands clutched at my back, fisting the fabric of my shirt. I touched her face gently, and kept my weight off of her even as she arched into me.

She was willing and clung to me as we kissed, but I was careful not to push her. I wanted her to set the pace even as my body demanded to have all of her.

I held her and kissed her with as much tenderness as I knew how to give. Her soft moans nearly undid me, but I aimed to show this woman how a man ought to treat her – like she was the most incredible woman on the face of the earth. And to me, she was.

I never wanted to stop kissing her, but we both needed to catch our breath, and I really had meant to show her the waterfall, not kiss her in the sand. Not that I regretted the way things turned out of course. We laid there for a moment, chests heaving, just holding each other.

I kissed her forehead and eased myself back to my feet. As I turned away, I adjusted myself in my jeans that were now about three sizes too small.

"Well, you ready to get in the water now?"

"I've already been in the water," she said and I could hear the teasing in her voice.

I glanced back at her and my breath caught to see her stretched out in the sand, her hair tousled, skirts skewed, and her lips perfectly plump and swollen from my attentions.

I cleared my throat and looked away. I heard her giggle, and when I chanced a look at her again, mischief danced in her eyes.

I liked this side of her.

"That's true." I shook my head at the thought of her feet flying into the air. "Good thing we're looking for rocks and not fish. I think you scared away all the fish in the county."

She gasped in mock indignation. "I thought it was a pretty graceful fall, all things considered."

At that, I did laugh. A deep, hearty laugh that I hadn't felt since Mary died.

"Fine," she huffed. "Let me get these blasted wet shoes off." She started tugging at the laces and I couldn't help chuckling at the look of frustration on her face. She was even prettier when she was mad.

"Need some help?"

"Yes, actually. This is all your fault, you know." She grumbled and stuck out her foot, as if daring me to help her.

"My fault?" I grinned, wondering where this line of thought would take us.

"Yes, you ... distracted me." Then she blushed furiously and looked away.

"And how exactly did I distract you?" I growled.

She squeaked. "Never mind, will you just help me get these off. Please."

"My lady, I'd do anything for you." I knelt in front of her and unlaced her boots slowly. The water made the laces swell and I took my time working the knots free. I could tell she hadn't expected such commitment to the task, and she blushed under my attentions. I eased one shoe off, then the other. I gently squeezed her calf as I trailed my other hand up to find the top of her stockings. Her legs tensed and I stopped, looking to her for permission. She searched my eyes for a moment, then relaxed her leg even as she clenched her hands in her skirts.

I trailed my fingers lightly along the underside of her thigh, just above her knee where I found the edge of her stockings. She gasped and I tucked my fingers under one stocking and slid it slowly down her leg. My other hand trailed over the exposed skin the stocking left behind. I tossed the stocking aside with her boots and repeated the process with her other leg. I loved how flustered she looked. Her breath came in quick gasps that had her breasts straining against her thin cotton dress. Her legs were slightly parted, and I knelt between them, one hand still on her ankle. I reached forward and snaked my arm around her waist, drawing her to me in a quick motion.

"Are you ready to get wet now?" I whispered in her ear, and the way she shivered against me was answer enough.

I stood and brought her up with me as if she weighed nothing. I stepped away and smirked when she whined a bit at the loss of me. Then she was pinning me with a look that clearly let me know she knew what I was doing, and I couldn't help the grin that stretched across my face.

I loved the fire in this woman.

With her eyes on me, she reached down and grasped the edge of her skirt. My mouth hung open as I watched her bring the hem up and tuck it into her waistband. She wasn't showing any more leg than I was, but somehow the sight of her with her skirt gathered up around her knees sent a new wave of lustful thoughts all through me.

Sierra batted her eyes as she walked toward me. She trailed a hand along my stomach as she headed for the water, her short nails ghosting along the ridges of my abdomen. Then she gave me a look that would star in my fantasies 'til the day I died.

"I'm already wet," she said. Her voice was rough with desire, and I stopped breathing.

This woman was going to kill me, and I would love every minute of it.

Sierra

THE RIDE back to the house was quiet, and I let myself enjoy the feeling of Tucker. I couldn't believe he kissed me. My lips still tingled. It was unlike anything I ever experienced before. He was gentle but confident, and I had opened myself to him.

Tucker helped me slide off Max when we got to the house, and then he was next to me. I could tell he wanted to hold me again. Maybe he even wanted to kiss me again. I hoped he would. He must have seen it in my eyes, because he leaned in and pressed his lips against mine.

This kiss was even better than the last. The anticipation had been building since we left the waterfall, and even though I was pressed against him the whole ride home, I was starved for his touch.

I forgot to breathe. My lungs burned, but I would choose kissing him over breathing any day. He kissed me hungrily, and it was the greatest pleasure in the world. He pulled away and I whined with need. Tucker grinned at me, his eyes sparkling with mischief. Then he lowered his mouth to my neck. He nipped and licked at my soft skin, and I arched back to give him better access. My toes curled. My soul quivered. He gripped me tight against him, and I was thankful for his strong arms. My legs refused to hold me any longer.

Tucker pulled back from my boneless body and placed one last gentle kiss on my lips. He pressed his forehead against mine and said, "As much as I'd like to stand here and kiss you all day, I should probably get a few things done." I felt him smile against my mouth. "Clint will be wondering what we were up to all day."

He laughed then, and I playfully batted at his chest. I forced my legs to hold me upright and smoothed my hands over my hair, but I was certain I looked thoroughly ravished.

"Go on, then." I playfully pushed him toward the horse pasture and made my way into the house, clutching the blue crystal in my hand. I never had a man give me anything except a hard time, but the whole trip to the waterfall had been a wonderful gift. This crystal in my hand meant more to me than Tucker would ever know.

I put it under my pillow and went about cleaning the house with a new sense of purpose and more energy than I'd had in forever. I even found an old recipe book and decided to make something fun. I knew I wasn't the world's best cook, or even this family's best cook, but I thought I was getting better. And I really wanted to bake a cake.

The sound of horses, wagon wheels, and laughter let me know the kids were home. I put a clean dish towel over the cake and tried to hide it out of sight on the counter. It had turned out better than I expected, and I hoped it tasted good too.

The kids came running to me when I stepped outside, their faces bright with excitement and ready to tell me all about their day. Clint hopped off the wagon and went over to Tucker. His movements seemed stiff, angry even, and I watched as the men talked by Storm's corral. I frowned at the tension on their faces. Their low voices didn't carry across the yard. I wanted to know what they were talking about, but the children were tugging at my hands begging to tell me about their day.

Clint probably had something to say about the

horses. I knew there was an auction coming up, and Tucker would drive the horses east in a day or two. I pushed my worries from my mind and looked at the pictures the children wanted to show me.

"Annie did the best drawing in the whole class. Missus May said so," Gracie said. They each had a folder with papers, and Tuck Junior had already spread his across the porch.

"I'd love to see it." Annie blushed at my attention and Gracie's words.

The older girl opened her folder and turned it toward me. My breath caught and my eyes blurred with tears. She had drawn all of us by the campfire. I was standing by Tucker, and she drew herself holding my hand, then Gracie and Tuck Junior all in a line. We were all smiling, and in the neatest writing I ever saw at the top of the page, she had written 'Family'.

"Oh, honey!" My voice cracked as I pulled her into a hug. "This is beautiful."

"Why are you crying if it's so beautiful?" Gracie asked.

"These are happy tears. I just love being here with you kids and your dad, and Annie's picture made me really happy."

Annie returned my hug with a fierce grip, and then Gracie and Junior piled on as well. I looked over the heads of the children and out to the corral where the men were still standing. I caught Tucker's gaze, and the fierceness in his eyes softened when he saw me with the children. He looked away, but I saw that he took a piece of paper from Clint and stuffed it in his pocket.

I frowned — my worries coming back tenfold.

"It's about time for dinner. Put your drawings in the house so you can show your dad later and go wash up." The kids scampered away, and I marched across the yard to see what had Tucker looking like he wanted to kick a door in.

He didn't look at me as I approached, and a knot formed in the pit of my stomach. My mind raced with possibilities, but I had no idea what news Clint brought that had them both looking like their favorite horse died.

"Is everything okay?" I touched Tucker's arm, and he jerked toward me as if he didn't know I was standing there. His face softened when he looked at me, and the knot in my stomach eased a little. Surely, they had just been talking business. There was a lot to do to get the horses to auction, and I knew Tucker stressed about getting everything done and ready to go.

"Nothing to worry about," he said. That wasn't the answer I expected.

"Is it something to do with the horses?" I pushed.

He was quiet for a long time, and I almost asked again when he reached in his pocket and pulled out the piece of paper he took from Clint.

"Clint visited with Tuff while he was in town. I don't want you to worry about this, because Tuff knows the truth and he's been taking these down whenever he sees them."

"Worry about what?" My hands shook as I took the paper from Tucker. I felt his eyes on my face as I unfolded it. I gasped and dropped the poster. My hands covered my mouth, and for the second time today tears filled my eyes.

But these were not happy tears.

The poster mocked me from the ground.

WANTED ALIVE

$500 REWARD
for the return of
SIERRA SUTTON

There was a drawing of me that was a good likeness. Anyone in town would probably know who this poster wanted. There was some more text about me breaking my contract and stealing, but I couldn't read anymore as my sight blurred with tears. A sob wracked my body, and then Tucker had me in his arms.

His hold was fierce. Protective. And I collapsed into him.

It was like every tear I ever held in was leaving my body all at once. I hadn't cried this hard since I was fifteen and my mother died. Jackson put me to work that same day.

I hadn't even cried after my first night with Preston. I turned off all my emotions after that night but being here with Tucker had awakened me again. I was starting to feel, to love, and now I worried it was all too good to last.

Maybe I wasn't meant to have a good life.

Slowly, I became aware of Tucker's voice. He was talking to me in soft tones, his lips moving against my hair. His chest rumbled against my ear as he talked about how everything was going to be okay. Then he hummed a little song that I only heard him sing once, when he thought he was alone.

My breathing slowed and my tears stopped. My face felt puffy and hot, and I was sure I looked a mess. I tried to wipe my face discreetly on my sleeve, not wanting Tucker to see me covered in snot. But when I pulled away, he caught my chin in a firm grip. He tilted my face up to his and kissed me right there. Right where Clint or the kids might have seen. Even though my eyes were swollen and my face was streaked with snot and tears. In that moment, I felt like we were the only two people in the world.

"You don't worry yourself one bit about this,

understand?" His voice was fierce, as if he could will away all my worries with the intensity of his words. "Tuff's a good man. A good sheriff. He won't let this get around. And I won't let anything happen to you. You're safe with me." He pulled me against him, and I nodded into his chest.

I did feel safe here. Safe with him. Safe in his arms.

But he didn't know Jackson, and he didn't know how far Preston McKlellan's money could stretch. And what it could buy.

Tucker

IT BROKE me to see her like this. She'd come so far and now her past, and those men, were trying to drag her back. Sierra belonged with me.

"Clint got this poster from Tuff," I told her. "There weren't any posted in town."

Sierra nodded. I hated that she seemed so lost. It was like her tears had put out the fire inside her that had just started to take hold.

"Look at me." I gripped her chin and forced her to meet my eyes. "Do you think I'll let anyone take you?"

She searched my eyes. "I know you'll try to stop

them, but you don't know these men, Tucker."

"I've known men like them." I didn't know what would happen, but I knew we weren't going to live in fear. I wasn't going to let Sierra live in fear. "And where do you think those men are now?"

I could see it in her eyes. She knew where they were. She knew I was dangerous from nearly the moment I met her, but she still wanted me. I didn't want her to think of me as a killer, but I wanted her to know I would kill to protect her.

"Dead," she whispered. "They're dead."

And I knew she didn't mean just the men from my past. She knew if any man came for her, they were already dead.

"Tuff will be by in a couple days. Said he owed you a visit anyway," Clint said. Sierra had gone back into the house, and we were supposed to be washing up for dinner, but my mind was a million miles away. Or maybe not quite a million. Just however many miles it was to Missouri and the men who thought Sierra belonged to them.

"Tuff's a good man," I said.

"Has Sierra said who put the reward out for her? It would help if we could give a name to Tuff."

"I'll ask her tomorrow. Not tonight. We better get

inside before the food gets cold." I imagined the saloon owner was one of the men. Jackson was his name, if I remembered correctly from that awful day in town when Harlan had shown Sierra's brand to everyone. I didn't want to ask her, but I knew she would know exactly who was looking for her. And when I had their names, I would be the one looking for them.

The kids had their drawings scattered across the room when we came in.

"What's all this?" I asked. "Did you do these at school?"

"Yep," Junior said. "Annie's is the best."

"Is that right?" I chuckled. "These all look good to me."

"But the teacher said Annie's really was the best," Gracie added.

"Oh, well where is this drawing then? Saving the best for last?" I reached out to tickle Gracie as she ran by me to get to the table. Sierra smiled as she set a basket of rolls on the table, and I was glad to see she looked better. She seemed almost relaxed, and it made my heart swell to think of the trust she was putting in me.

Annie produced her painting shyly, and Sierra looked away with a blush. I wondered why she was blushing as I looked at the picture. Was she worried about my reaction? Annie had done a great job capturing the night we all spent by the campfire.

"This is wonderful, Annie." I hugged my oldest, but my eyes were on Sierra. I could tell she relaxed the tiniest bit at my words. Maybe she was worried I thought we weren't a family yet. I would make sure she knew that I counted her part of this family even before we kissed.

"Hey! Why am I not in this picture?" Clint held a hand to his heart in mock indignation. The kids giggled.

"Oh, Uncle Clint, Tuckie drew you in his picture," Gracie said. I nudged one of the drawings toward my ranch hand. His eyes bugged out.

"Why is my head so big? And where are my arms?"

The kids broke down in laughter, and I caught Sierra hiding a laugh as she brought out another pan.

"Okay, children." She pinned her gaze on Clint too. "Let's say the blessing, then we can eat. I have a surprise for after dinner."

"A surprise?" Junior's eyes lit up, and he squirmed in his seat with excitement.

"What is it?" Annie asked.

"Well, it wouldn't be a surprise if I told you," Sierra said. "But you won't have to wait long. If Clint will say the blessing, I'll show you the surprise. But you still have to wait until after dinner for it."

I think Clint wanted to find out what the mysterious surprise was as much as the kids, because he said the fastest blessing I ever heard from him. After a chorus of Amens, the kids looked at Sierra expectantly.

"I baked a cake." She set the pan down on the table and pulled the cloth off it.

"Oooh!" The children and Clint exclaimed. Junior clapped his hands.

"Is it somebody's birthday?" Gracie asked.

"No, not that I know of." Sierra looked at me as she answered, and I shook my head. "I just wanted to do something fun for you kids, and I thought a cake sounded pretty fun."

"Cake is so fun," Gracie agreed.

Everyone ate their dinner quickly so they could have cake, but I noticed Sierra just pushed her food around on her plate. Maybe she wasn't feeling quite back to herself yet. I would just have to fix that.

When everyone had some cake and complimented Sierra's baking skills at least twenty times, I had an idea.

"You know what's almost as much fun as cake?" Everyone looked at me. "A ghost hunt with Uncle Clint." Even though Clint wasn't a relative, the kids had taken to calling him Uncle and it stuck.

"Yes! Can we, Uncle Clint, can we?" Annie asked. She didn't usually ask for things, so I knew that would tug at his already pretty soft heart.

"Sure, but if we see a real ghost, you're on your own." Clint scooped up another piece of cake and shoved his hat on his head as he headed to the front door. "Last one out's a rotten egg."

The kids shrieked and ran past him to scramble into the wagon.

"Reckon it might take us a while to find a ghost this evening." Clint winked at me, then tipped his hat to Sierra. He closed the door behind him, and I heard him shout, "Everybody needs a lantern!"

"Will they be okay?" Sierra came up beside me to look out the front window. Lanterns bobbed back and forth across the yard as the kids chased Clint.

"They don't go very far. Usually just down to the field by the horses, but the kids like hanging out with Clint."

"I just worry about them being out in the woods at night," she said.

"Clint won't let them get that far. They'll stay near the horses in the valley. Not very far away at all." I stepped closer to Sierra and brushed a loose curl away from her face. I let my hand linger on her cheek. "But just far enough."

"Far enough for what?" She looked up at me shyly, her cheeks turning pink as I watched her.

"Anything you want," I said. I wasn't going to push her or do anything she wasn't ready for, and if all she wanted was to be held, then I would hold her. But if she wanted more than that, then I could do that too.

She stared at her feet and picked at the sleeve of her dress. I cupped her cheek and smoothed my thumb over her lips. She leaned into my touch.

"You sure you want a woman like me?" She turned her head and brought her hands up to push away from me. I caught them in my hand and held them against my chest.

"What's that supposed to mean?"

"You know exactly what I mean," she laughed bitterly.

"You're kind and strong and patient. And loving. And beautiful." I could think of so many more words to describe her. "Any man would be lucky to have a woman like you."

"Any man has had me." Her voice cracked.

"Stop." I turned her towards me and forced her to look at me. "What happened to you in your past wasn't your fault, and it doesn't make think any less of you. You're the best thing to happen to me in a long time."

"I doubt that." She let out a self-deprecating laugh.

"It's true. After Mary died," I paused. I didn't talk about Mary much with Sierra because I didn't want her to think she was being compared to my first wife. "Ever since Mary died, it's the kids that kept me going. I've just been going through the motions. Alive, but not living. But you ... you changed something in me. I haven't felt the same since I first saw you at the train station. You awoke something in me I never thought I'd feel again. I care about you. "

"I never thought I'd find someone that cared about

me — someone I could care about too," she whispered. "I never thought I'd find a man like you."

"And what kind of man am I?" I hoped with all my heart that she was falling for me as hard as I was for her, but now I felt like a schoolboy talking to his crush. I was equal parts excited and terrified to know exactly what she thought of me.

"A good man," she said.

"I've done bad things…terrible things." She needed to know the truth. I wanted a future with her, but just like she worried about her past — I worried about mine. "I've killed men, Sierra. You saw me in town. I'll kill again, if I need to."

"You don't scare me." Her shyness was gone now, and she stepped even closer, tilting her head back to look up at me. "We both come from dark pasts."

"I'm not as good as you." I murmured against her lips.

"You're the best thing that ever happened to me too, Tucker West," she breathed into me. And then I was lost in her.

Sierra

I HAD WORRIED my past would cloud my life with Tucker, but as he took me in his arms, it felt like I was held for the very first time. His arms wrapped around me, and I could feel the heat of him through my dress. His chest pressed into mine as leaned into me, and I felt the rough cabin wall against my back. But he didn't push. He didn't hurt. He just held me.

I didn't feel scared or used. I felt treasured.

He dipped his head toward mine and when our lips met it was deep and gentle. I wrapped my arms around his neck then ran my fingers through his hair. I'd never explored a man like this. I'd never wanted to. But Tucker was different from any man I'd ever known. And I couldn't get enough of it.

His lips left mine and he began a slow trail of kisses down my neck. His breath was warm against my tender skin and leaned my head back to give him more room.

I wanted more.

I wanted everything.

His strong hands stroked down my back to rest on my hips. He squeezed gently and pressed his body closer to mine as he nuzzled my neck.

"Tucker," I gasped.

He pulled back and looked at me, his dark eyes shining with want.

"Are you good?" He asked. His thumbs rubbed small circles on my hips.

I nodded and felt my face flush with happiness. I bit my lip, and he brought a hand up to my face. He smoothed his thumb over my lip then cupped my face.

I loved the feel of his rough hands on my skin. I leaned into his touch, and he smiled.

I ran my hands over his shoulders and down the front of his chest. I paused at his waistband then gently tugged at his shirt where it was tucked into his pants. He inhaled sharply and growled low in his throat, but then he brought his hands over mine and stilled them.

I paused, suddenly embarrassed. Maybe he didn't

want me the way I wanted him. Had I misread him? Did he think me wanton?

"I'm sorry." I tried to pull away but he held onto me.

"Nothing to be sorry about." His voice sounded strained. "I should be apologizing to you."

I knew it. He was going to say it had all been a mistake and he didn't mean to lead me on. When he said he cared about me, he hadn't meant like this. I could feel the tears already forming in my eyes. I blinked rapidly to keep them from falling.

"I didn't mean to come on so strong. You're one hell of a woman, Sierra, and I want to do this right."

"I...what? I don't understand." I took a deep breath and finally met his eyes. He touched my face and wiped away a stray tear with his thumb.

"Did I upset you? I didn't mean to move so fast." He took a small step back and searched my face. Clearly looking for any sign he'd overstepped.

"No, not at all," I laughed at my foolishness. "I thought you were going to say this was all a mistake." I gestured vaguely at myself and wiped at my face.

"Never. I don't regret anything unless I've pushed you too fast."

"No," I said quickly. "No, you haven't done anything I haven't wanted." Then I felt the heat in my face at my admission. Tucker laughed quietly.

"Good because I want to do this right. If it's alright with you, I'd like to court you properly."

"Court me?" I'd never known anyone who'd been courted before. I didn't even know what it meant entirely.

"Court you." Tucker smirked at the expression on my face. "I'd like to take you out and watch the stars, or go on a picnic, maybe take a day trip to Harper Hill. It's the next town over and they have the finest dress shop in the area. You could pick out a dress or whatever else you'd like. If you want."

I gaped at him, and he seemed suddenly unsure of himself.

"If you –"

"Yes," I interrupted him and couldn't help the smile on my face. "It all sounds lovely."

"Good." He smiled. "That's good." Then he sighed and drew me in close. I wrapped my arms around him, and he held me like that for a long while. I felt his lips move against my hair, but he didn't do more than hold me.

I closed my eyes and breathed him in. I desired him more in this moment than in all the moments before. I'd never been treasured by a man in such a way, and the feeling of it lit a fire in my belly that I didn't think would ever go out.

"You better court me fast, Tucker West." The words came out without thought and I flushed from my head to my toes as I felt the chuckle rumble through his chest.

"We can go as fast or as slow as you like," he said.

I hummed my acceptance and thought of all the ways I wanted to know this man better. I wanted to know him in mind and body, but it seemed I'd have to hold off on knowing his body too well. I laughed at that and finally pulled away from Tucker's embrace.

"What's so funny?" His eyes shined in the flickering light of the oil lanterns.

"Just thinking about what we can do since you're such a gentleman."

He laughed at that, and I thought I saw the slightest blush on his face.

"Will you teach me to play checkers?" The kids seemed to love the game, and I'd never learned to play. It didn't seem particularly hard, but still, it would be nice to learn the rules. It would be nice to have Tucker teach me.

"Haven't you learned by now, I'll give you anything you want?" He reached above the fireplace to get the box of checkers off the mantle.

"Well, you haven't quite given me *everything* I want."

He coughed and cleared his throat, and there was no mistaking the blush on his face.

"I'll be giving you things you didn't know you wanted when the time comes," he said, and then it was my turn to blush.

He moved the small side table in front of the fireplace and set two chairs from the kitchen beside it. I sat across from him as he laid out the checkerboard and divided the checkers between us. Tucker's low voice rumbled pleasantly through the quiet room as he explained the game, and I was pleased to learn it was nearly as simple as it looked. The fire crackled and popped as we played and after losing three games, I finally captured all of Tucker's checkers in the fourth game.

"Reckon that's a good way to end it." He chuckled. "What do you say about me taking you outside and showing you some stars?" He grinned and waggled his eyebrows comically.

I laughed. "Why Tucker West, are you courting me already?"

"Might be." He grabbed my waist and swept me in close.

"Then I think that sounds lovely." I placed my hands on his chest and tried not to think about how much his shirt was in the way. He kissed my forehead and grabbed a blanket off the back of a chair. He wrapped the blanket around my shoulders as we stepped onto the porch.

The sky stretched vast and dark from one end of the valley to the other. The mountains rose like midnight sentries guarding the lands below. I gasped at the number of stars. Like crystals under the falls, they were more numerous and sparkled more brightly.

"It's beautiful," I breathed.

"Reckon we should spend more time out here at night." Tucker scooted the rocking chairs close together and we sat.

"It's easy to forget to enjoy things, especially when you assume it will always be there."

"It's easy to stay busy," Tucker agreed. He sighed and looked off in the distance.

I nodded and wondered if he was thinking of his first wife. We hadn't spoken of her much and I didn't want to pry. I didn't like to think of my being here as taking her place, but she was part of Tucker as much as my past was a part of me.

I ran my hand along the back of Tucker's head and rubbed his neck. I felt the raised skin of a scar just below his hairline.

"How'd you get this?" I couldn't help asking even though I dreaded any queries into my own scars. Tucker's past was a mystery to me and while this scar could have been from handling horses, something told me it wasn't.

"Bullet grazed me in California. The guy was a sneaky bastard, but a shit shot, lucky for me. Not so lucky for him."

"You're lucky you aren't dead," I said.

"Just a hazard of the job," he said. I raised an eyebrow at that, but I doubted he could see my reaction in the shadowed darkness of the porch.

Tucker reached for me and rubbed his thumb over the palm of my hand. His fingers traced lazy circles along my hand and wrist. I enjoyed the sensation, not even thinking about the brand on my wrist until his fingers grazed the scarred ridges of it. He paused and his whole form went rigid.

"Does it hurt?" he asked.

"Not anymore." In fact, the skin of my wrist was numb to all sensation.

"I'm sorry."

"Not your fault, just a hazard of the job." I parroted his words back to him.

He clenched his jaw, and I could feel the anger rolling off him, "If I ever see the man who did that, I'll –"

I cupped his face to shush him. "That's all in the past now. With any luck I'll never see Jackson again. Hopefully he'll die of some venereal disease and his dick will fall off."

Tucker laughed at that, and I felt some of the tension leave his body. We sat in silence for a while longer, watching the clouds roll across the moon. The wind had a chill to it that promised winter would soon arrive, but the night was pleasant.

The horses nickered in the far field and I could see their shadowed forms moving against the base of the mountain as they played and kicked at each other. The valley was full of horses but would soon be much emptier when Tucker drove some to the auction. I knew the auction was close, maybe only days away, but I hadn't liked to think on it. Still, it was something that needed to happen whether I worried or not.

"When do you take the horses to auction?" I knew Tucker had to go, but I dreaded the thought of him leaving me, even for a night.

"Supposed to ride out tomorrow, but I can push it 'til tomorrow evening and still make it in time." He sighed, and I could hear him thinking. "I don't want to leave you here alone. If I push the horses, I can be back by the day after tomorrow, but I'll have to take Clint with me to make that work."

"I'd be lying if I said I wasn't worried about you leaving. But we will be okay for one night and half the day."

"There's another auction in a few months. I could just wait and take the horses to that one," he mused.

"In the dead of winter? I'll not have you risking your neck or livelihood by driving horses through the mountains in the middle of winter."

"Smart too," he whispered. "I think I forgot to say that earlier. I love you because you're smart ,too."

I laughed.

"Isn't Tuff coming out soon anyway? He'll be here tomorrow or the next day to check on things.

"It still makes me nervous."

"What if Clint stays? Can you take the horses on

your own?" I didn't like the idea of Tucker going alone, but it would make us both feel better if someone was here with us.

"I could. I've done it before. It just takes longer, but if Clint was here with you, then an extra night wouldn't hurt anything. I just wouldn't take Storm."

I knew the big stallion had calmed down a lot since I arrived, but he was still skittish and high-strung. I heard Clint and Tucker discussing whether to take him to the auction even if they were both driving the horses. A stallion could really mess with the herd.

"I don't like it entirely, since you'll still be leaving me, but I do feel better knowing Clint will be here. And you're sure you can handle the horses alone?" I did trust him in this. I knew Tucker didn't take chances with the health of his horses. He wouldn't try to drive them if he was worried.

"I'll be fine. No stallions or new foals, just some gentle mares and a few yearlings." Tucker pulled me tight against him. "And I'll feel better too. I'll still get back quick as I can."

"You'll be leaving early tomorrow, so you better get some sleep," I said. "Do you think Clint will be back with the kids soon?"

"Any minute now, I reckon." Tucker stood and leaned against the porch post. I couldn't help but admire his broad shoulders and the way his jeans hugged him in all the right places.

"Enjoying the view?" Tucker grinned at me and I blushed having been caught obviously checking out his backside.

"Yes, in fact I was. The valley is very pretty at night," I said with as much indignation as I could muster.

Tucker laughed at that and then we heard more laughter in the distance along with the jangle of a horse harness.

I stood by Tucker as the wagon came into view, the children's lanterns bobbing happily in the darkness. It sounded like they were all singing a song and I wrapped my arms around Tucker.

I didn't know when I had ever felt more happy in my life.

I just hoped I could hold on to this feeling forever.

Tucker

I SLEPT better than I expected despite my worry. I had an idea of what had helped my sleep, and I smiled at the memory of the night before. I didn't know the last time I'd had such a relaxing evening and kissing Sierra had certainly been good for my soul. But my worries came back to me as soon as I woke. I decided to get started packing for my trip. The sky was still gray when I pulled on my boots, and I was surprised to find Sierra already sitting on the porch.

"I made coffee," she said when I came out the front door.

I leaned over to kiss the top of her head. She smiled into her mug. She looked so cute curled up in the chair, wrapped in a big quilt with her hands curled around her mug of coffee. I just wanted to sit and drink coffee with her all day.

I needed to get the horses to auction, but I hated the idea of leaving Sierra while the reward posters were still floating around. I trusted Tuff to keep them off the bulletin board in town, but these things had a way of spreading.

At least Clint would be here. I still needed to tell my ranch hand the change of plans.

"You need some more shooting practice before I go." We had practiced a few more times and Sierra was getting better, but she was still nervous. She hit the target more often than not, but she still flinched when she pulled the trigger. I knew the little pistol still made her anxious, and not because she feared guns.

"I wouldn't want to wake the kids," she said.

I shrugged. "They can sleep through anything. Come on, it'll be fun."

She rolled her eyes but unfolded herself from the blanket. "I don't know about fun, but it will be cold."

I laughed and pulled her to me. "I'll keep you warm."

"You better." She tilted her head up to look at me, and I couldn't help kissing her.

"Ahem."

Sierra pulled away from me, her face nearly as red as her dress. Clint stood just off the porch, rocking on his heels and grinning like the devil he was.

"Mornin'," he said. "Just wanted a cup of coffee. Don't let me interrupt."

Sierra mumbled a greeting as Clint stepped around us and into the house. When she looked at me, we both laughed. She covered her face with her hands, and I pulled her to me again. Then I took her hand and led her to our makeshift shooting range.

"I think you're ready to handle the big pistol." I unholstered my six-shooter and handed it to her.

"I'll never know how you shoot this one-handed." Sierra struggled to hold it steady with both hands. "I don't think I can do it."

"Sure you can." I leaned in close and adjusted her stance by pushing a little on one of her hips. Her foot moved and her posture shifted. "That's better. Remember to breathe and hold 'er steady."

She huffed out a breath but didn't complain anymore. She squeezed the trigger, and the gun went off with a crack that echoed across the still valley. The gun jerked in her hands, but she didn't drop it and it didn't knock her in the head, either.

"That's my girl." I pointed at the target. "That's the best yet. Almost a bullseye."

Sierra let out a surprised little laugh and held the gun up again for a second shot. She popped off four more shots and hit the target every time.

"You been practicing without me?" She was shooting so much better than I expected. I knew using my pistol would be a struggle for her, but she was rising to the challenge.

"Just been dreaming about shooting Preston McKlellan right between the eyes," she muttered.

I stilled. She never mentioned any names before, and this one sounded familiar because I knew him. He owned half of Kansas, or at least acted like he did. Tomorrow I would be delivering my horses to his auction.

"Are you okay?" Sierra lowered the pistol and turned to me.

"You never said a name before." She stiffened at my words, her eyes wary. "What was his name?"

"He said I was his, and he wouldn't let another man have me. He paid Jackson enough that it was true. Some of the other girls thought I was lucky." She laughed, but there was no humor in the sound. "Lucky to have the attentions of Preston McKlellan. But they didn't see him behind closed doors. No, I'll be lucky the day he's dead." She turned away from me and raised the pistol. There was no hesitation in her movements. Her hands were steady when she pulled the trigger.

Bullseye.

I gently took the gun from her and spoke as I reloaded it. "I know him."

She went still as the mountain ice, her face white as the first snow. I took a step past her and faced the target. I sent all six shots into the target before my mind knew my hands were moving. The shots echoed down the valley long after I holstered the gun.

"I never cared for the man. Been wanting a reason to shoot him."

"How do you know him?" Her voice was barely more than a whisper.

"He runs the auction where I take the horses. I only talked with him a few times. Too much of a smooth talker for me. Walked in on him berating a stable hand once. Reckon he would have whipped the boy if I hadn't been there."

"He wasn't much for talking," Sierra said. "I knew he was rich because he liked to show off his money, but other than talking about his cattle and riding in on a different stallion about every week, I didn't know what he did."

"Reckon the cattle are where he has most of his money, but the horses don't hurt. His auction is the biggest this side of the Mississippi."

"What are you going to do?"

I stared at the horizon where the sky was turning pink with the rising sun. I didn't want to throw away the life I built here, but it wouldn't be much of a life if I was always looking over my shoulder. I was a vigilante before, and it scared me how easy it felt to take on that role again.

"I have some horses to sell," I said. "Then I have some killin' to do."

"No." Sierra clung to my arm. "If he comes here, then you can deal with him, but you'll be arrested if you kill him."

"They have to catch me first, and I've never been caught." My blood was boiling at the thought of Preston McKlellan running his auction all these years with that smug smile on his face, then spending his nights with Sierra. Hurting her. Doing whatever he wanted without a thought for her. I knew he was a snake, but if I had known he mistreated women, I would have killed him a long time ago.

"Please, Tucker, think of your kids." Her eyes welled with tears. She looked beautiful in the morning sun, and I ran my thumb over her cheek to wipe away a tear. "Think of me."

"All I do is think about you," I said, but some of the fight went out of me. I sighed and shook my head. "You're right, I have to think about our lives here. I don't like it, but I won't kill him tomorrow." Maybe the next day, but not tomorrow.

Sierra sagged against me, her small hands clenched in my shirt, and she buried her face in my chest.

"I'll say goodbye to the children, then I better head out. Sooner I leave, the sooner I can get back to you."

She nodded against me, then pulled away and walked up the hill. I watched her walk away, and my worry about leaving her for two nights came back with a vengeance. Now that I knew who was after her, I was nervous. Preston was beyond rich, and the reward money was pocket change to him. Preston's name wasn't on the poster. He had a reputation to uphold of course. But what he was really buying with that money was whispers and attention. Everyone would be looking for Sierra, and I worried the people in town might start talking.

I trusted Tuff to keep the posters out of sight as much as he could, but he couldn't be everywhere, and I knew Harlan and his men would be the first in line to try and claim the reward.

I didn't walk directly to the house. I walked around to the barn so I could talk with Clint before leaving. He was already outside fiddling with a broken rail on the corral. Storm watched him from a short distance away, but the big stallion was simply interested. Not too long ago, the stallion would have been eying both of us with rage. The horse had mellowed a lot as he got to know us, but he was still high strung.

"Storm kick that loose again?" I leaned against the fence next to Clint.

"Looks like it. The nails are rusted through. I'll have to get more in town." He nodded to the other side of the corral. "Couple more came loose over there, too. Maybe not entirely big Storm's fault. He doesn't kick nearly as much as he used to."

"Still, he kicks a little too much to take to auction. Besides, he's growing on me." I hadn't planned to keep the ornery stallion, but he was beautiful.

"The horses are ready, and Max is saddled. Just need to add your saddle bags." Clint met my eyes, and I knew he had something more to say.

"Go on, tell me what's on your mind."

"Heard you shootin' this morning," he said. "I think I should be asking what's on your mind."

I picked a long stem of grass and chewed on it.

"Preston McKlellan is on my mind." I spat on the ground.

"The horse auction guy?" Clint had been with me to the auction a few times, and he was even better at remembering names and faces than I was.

"He put out the reward on Sierra," I said.

"Shit."

I nodded. "Reckon I can't shoot him when I take the horses, but I want too."

"I should go with you."

"No, I need you here." I knew Clint wanted to

come and be my voice of reason. He knew even though I said I couldn't shoot Preston, I would still think about it. And sometimes, if I thought about something long enough, it had a way of happening.

"Just don't lose your head." And I knew Clint meant that in more than one way. Don't lose my cool and don't lose my head, literally.

"I'll say bye to the kids, then be on my way."

"Do I need to take the kids on a wagon ride so you can say goodbye to a certain someone?" Clint waggled his eyebrows at me, and I was glad for the teasing to break the tension.

I shook my head and was surprised to feel my face grow warm at the thought of how I would like to say goodbye to Sierra.

Clint laughed, "You got it bad, boss."

"Don't call me that," I grumbled, but I couldn't help grinning. "I want to spend the rest of my life with her, Clint."

Clint whistled. "She's good for you, and you're good for her."

I nodded. "Thank you. For everything. You've always had my back."

"Aw shucks, boss. You're gonna make me cry," Clint teased, but I could tell he was thinking about the past. All the things we had faced together. Now we had something else to face, and I was leaving. It didn't feel right, but there wasn't anything I could do about it.

"Just be careful while I'm gone. Keep the guns loaded, and –"

"And the horses saddled," Clint finished for me. "You be careful too."

"Always am," I said, and it was true. Being careful just meant taking care in the things I was doing, and I did everything with care.

Especially killing.

Sierra

DARK CLOUDS rolled in as Tucker drove his herd of horses out of the valley. The clouds seemed to chase him down the mountain, leaving darkness and emptiness in their wake. The sky churned, growing deeper and darker even as I watched. Lightning flashed high in the distance, and thunder rolled through the valley.

"Best get inside," Clint said. He was still trying to fix Storm's corral with things we had on hand. He didn't want to leave me to go into town while Tucker was gone. "I'll get the wagon in the barn and check on the horses."

"Come on kids, let's get inside before the storm hits." I just hoped Tucker traveled faster than this storm or stayed out of its path entirely. The clouds quickly turned the bright morning dark, and I lit lanterns inside the house. Annie sat by the fire with a book while the younger two played with blocks. I stood at the window and watched the wind whip the trees and long grass in the valley. Clint ran across the yard to the barn, then a moment later he was latching the barn door and heading for the house.

The shutter slammed across the window, and I jumped. Clint's boots were heavy on the porch as he shuttered all the windows across the front of the house. Then I heard the shutters on the back of the house slam shut, and the back door flew open as Clint came inside.

"I could have helped with the shutters." I felt like all Tucker and Clint ever did was take care of me. "I didn't know the storm would be this bad."

Clint waved me off. "It's no trouble, and hopefully it won't be too bad. But better to be safe than have broken windows." He hung up his coat and hat, then sat down at the kitchen table. Luckily the rain hadn't started yet, so he was dry. He was just cold from the wind and sudden drop in temperature.

"Here, let me heat the coffee." I needed to keep busy or else my mind would think about all the things that could go wrong. We didn't need a storm on top of everything else. "Will the horses be okay?"

"They're smart. Most were already up under the trees along the base of the mountain. There are some rocks that will protect them there, too. We've had a few good storms since I've been here and never lost one yet. They get loose sometimes, but I've always brought 'em back."

I nodded as I set the pot of coffee on the stove. I didn't want to ask about Tucker, but I couldn't help it.

"And will Tucker be okay in the storm?"

"Reckon he'll stay ahead of it," Clint said. "Good thing he left early."

I nodded again and started measuring out flour to make bread. I was still new to breadmaking, so it was a task that would keep my mind and hands busy for a few hours. While I waited for the bread to rise, there was plenty of cleaning, sock mending, and a million other things to do.

"Sierra." I froze when Clint said my name. "He'll be okay. Tuck's been through worse than a little rain."

I nodded but didn't turn to face him. I wanted to say I was worried about more than just the storm, but I didn't trust my voice and I didn't want to cry in front of the children. There was one window in the kitchen that didn't have a shutter over it. It was round and small and well-covered by the porch. I watched the storm roll in through this small window and flinched when lightning flashed outside. It was followed quickly by the crack of thunder. The whole house shook, and the kids screamed.

"That was close," Clint murmured.

"Everything's okay, children," I said. "Just some thunder and lightning. Probably be more of that before this storm is through." Calming the children took my mind off my own fears. I could be strong for them. I had to be.

"How about a game?" Clint asked the kids. A chorus of yeses had him pulling down the board games. He spread out backgammon and checkers. I poured Clint a cup of coffee as he got the kids set up with games. He sat down to play with them.

"Will you play with us Sierra?" Annie asked.

"Oh." Even though Tucker had taught me to play checkers, I always had something to keep me busy when the children played. Now, I felt guilty even thinking about enjoying myself while Tucker was potentially braving the storm with a herd of horses. "Maybe later. Let me finish making the bread, and then I have some cleaning to do."

Annie slumped a little in her chair, and a pang of sadness pierced me. I didn't expect my answer to disappoint her so much. I just wasn't used to the children, or anyone really, looking forward to spending time with me. I never had time for that at the saloon, and even though I counted Charity and Maggie as friends, we never sat and played games. I watched the men play poker sometimes, but I didn't have any real interest in cards. But I had enjoyed playing checkers with Tucker.

I opened my mouth, but before I could say a word, lightning exploded outside. The whole house shook again, and a picture fell off the wall. It crashed to the floor and the children screamed. Clint was up and looking out the front door before I fully processed what happened.

"Shit." He pulled on his coat and hat and ran outside. I caught the door before it closed and gasped at what I saw.

The barn was on fire.

"Children, I need to help Clint in the barn. Stay inside until we get back." I pulled on one of Tucker's extra coats. Luckily, I still had my boots on. I hurried across the yard, the bitter wind whipping at my face and hands. The rain hadn't started yet.

Clint brought out Colonel and started yelling when he saw me. "Tie Colonel to the post. We have to get the other horses out." I grabbed hold of the rope Tucker had thrown over Colonel's head and led the sturdy horse to the hitching post in front of the house. I tied him quickly and rushed back for the next horse. The mares and the wagon were all that was left in the barn, and the fire wasn't catching hold as quickly as I thought it would. Still, thick black smoke belched out of the loft window. The dappled mare was spooked when I took her from Clint.

"Easy, Julie," I tried to soothe her but my voice barely carried over the wind and thunder.

I hurried to tie her alongside Colonel and rushed

back one more time. I could see Clint through the barn door struggling with the big bay mare. He was trying to hitch her to the wagon, but she was too nervous. Smoke seeped down from the loft, and the back of the barn glowed orange with smoldering flames.

I rushed in and grabbed hold of the wagon's tongue.

"Can we move it together?" I yelled over the crackling of the timbers overhead.

Clint released the mare, and she galloped outside. He went to the back of the wagon and started to push. I pulled with everything in me, and slowly the wagon started to move. Too slowly.

The barn was suffocating with heat and smoke now. I heard Clint coughing, and my own throat itched. My eyes watered so badly, I could barely see the open doors.

Clint roared as he heaved against the wagon.

We needed to get out.

Wagons could be replaced, but we couldn't.

"Clint, we need to go!" I yelled at him, and the smoke clogged my mouth and nose. I felt the wagon surge behind me, and I scrambled to keep pulling. To keep moving forward.

Once we got it moving, I was nearly running to the door.

We were going to make it. The thought surged through me as the doors loomed closer, the promise of fresh air in sight. Then something crashed down from overhead, and Clint cried out. I had the full weight of the wagon, but momentum kept me moving forward. I ran through the doors and when the wagon was clear, I dropped the tongue. I didn't wait to see if the wagon stopped before I ran back into the barn.

Clint was on his hands and knees. He was dazed and coughing. I grabbed his arm and threw it over my shoulders. I gripped him around the waist and urged him toward the doors. He stumbled along, leaning heavily on me. My legs felt wooden. I half dragged Clint to the exit. My body shook with the effort.

Flames exploded to my left. A beam fell into the empty stall, and fire quickly engulfed the dry straw.

I shrieked, and with one last surge of adrenaline, heaved us both through the barn doors. We collapsed in the grass outside, but I could still feel the heat of the fire at my back. I struggled to my feet and put my hands under Clint's arms. I heaved and tried to drag him backwards. He kicked with his feet, helping propel himself with me.

I fell back on my bottom and took in great gulping breaths of air. I looked down at Clint where he was sprawled across my legs. He was rubbing at his face and tugging at his shirt.

"Clint, can you hear me?" I pushed his hat out of the way to see if he had been struck by something in the barn.

"That was..." Clint gasped for air, his words broken by another coughing fit. "...too close."

I nodded and nearly cried with relief. We were going to be okay. I looked toward the house where the two horses were tied, and beyond that, to the front door where three little faces peered out. The children were pale, and I could tell they were scared.

"Let's get you inside, then I'll take the horses to the shed behind the house." Clint nodded at my words, and I knew he must feel awful if he was agreeing to go inside while the horses still needed tending. I helped him up and he carried most of his own weight as we trudged across the yard.

I set him down in a chair just inside the door and told the children I would be right back.

I didn't know where the other mare had run off to, but I hoped she would seek out the other horses in the valley. I untied the two horses from the hitching post and led them down the hill to the small shed. It was open on one side, but deep enough to keep the horses safe from the worst of the storm.

I slipped the rope off Colonel and then heard the first drops of rain hit the shed roof.

"Great," I muttered. I dashed out of the shed and caught the rain. It came down in buckets and I was soaked through by the time I reached the back door and threw myself inside.

"Sierra!" The children cried out when I came through the door. They rushed toward me, their little arms open wide.

"Shh, shh, it's okay. We're all okay," I murmured as I held them. "Let me get changed into something dry, and then we'll all sit by the fire. I'll even play some checkers with you." A few moments before, I wanted nothing to do with fire ever again, but now my teeth were chattering and my bones felt cold. I checked on Clint before changing. He still sat by the open front door, breathing in great gulps of fresh air.

"The horses are safe," I told him. "Though I don't know where the other mare got to."

He nodded. "I'll find her tomorrow." His voice was rough. I noticed blood on the back of his neck. I hoped it was just from a scratch and not from a blow to his head.

"I'm going to change, then I can tend to you. Will you be okay for a few minutes?"

He nodded, and then pointed out the open door.

"Thank the Lord." I breathed out the words as I watched the rain pour down on the barn. Steam rose from the tin roof — what was left of it — and soon there was more smoke than flames licking at the oak boards.

The storm wasn't over, but it felt like we had passed through the worst of it.

I prayed Tucker got through it okay, too. It seemed like my worries just kept piling up, and I needed some good news for a change.

Tucker

THE STORM clouds followed me south, but when I headed east toward Kansas, I managed to avoid the worst of it. The horses were hardy and didn't mind a little rain. Can't say the same for me, but I survived. I was cold and wet when I stopped to camp.

The horses didn't need much rest, and I hoped I could get started again before dawn. If I kept up the pace, we would get to the auction by midday. Then I would wait around for the sale on the following day and head back late. With any luck, I could make it home before dark on the third day. I was glad I left Clint with Sierra and the kids. Even though I was to be gone three nights or more, I wasn't as worried knowing he was there to watch over things. I would have preferred to stay and send Clint on this mission, but I knew he wasn't that comfortable herding the horses on his own.

After checking the horses one more time, I laid my bedroll by the small fire and stretched out to sleep. Max grazed nearby. I didn't like sleeping out in the open, but I trusted Max to alert me to anything sneaking around.

I closed my eyes and willed sleep to come. I just wanted this trip to be over and head back to the ranch.

Back to Sierra.

I woke well before dawn. I choked down some hard tack while checking on the horses and packing up my little camp. Then I saddled Max and loaded my saddle bags. I didn't sleep well, and my body was tense with nervous energy.

Max must have sensed it, because he danced away from me and turned in a circle when I tried to mount him. I hauled myself up in the saddle and took him in a big loop around the herd. He tossed his head and pulled at the bit, wanting to go faster.

"Easy, boy." I patted his neck. "We both need to try and relax."

When I was satisfied that all the horses were fit and ready to go, I urged them East toward the Kansas border. I hoped we would cross into Kansas before first light and then have plenty of time to reach the stockyard before noon.

If luck was really on my side, I might get the horses into the sale tonight.

The ride was slow and uneventful. Once the sun came up, the scenery unfolded flat and grassy as far as I could see. It gave me a lot of time to think. Too much time to think.

I worried about the ranch and Clint and the kids, but most of all I worried about Sierra. I didn't like that Preston was after her. I imagined all the ways I could make him pay for the things he did. All the ways I could make him hurt the way Sierra hurt.

I couldn't imagine treating any woman the way he did. Especially not one as beautiful and gentle as Sierra.

Just the thought of her filled me with a warmth I couldn't express in words. I hadn't felt like this since Mary. I hoped if Mary was looking down on me now, she would approve of me courting Sierra. I would never forget Mary, and I'd always love her, but I needed a woman in my life as much as the kids did. We all needed Sierra.

I smiled at the thought of our first kiss...and second and third. Imagining all the ways I wanted to make love to her was a good distraction from worrying. I felt myself growing hard at the thought of her softness against me. The feel of her lips. The fire in her eyes.

I couldn't wait to get home and start courting her properly. I smiled at the thought of buying her a dress and taking her out to dinner. I kept my mind busy thinking of all the ways I would show Sierra how much she meant to me as the miles disappeared beneath Max's hooves.

I was tired and saddle sore by the time I caught the first whiff of the stockyard. They said the smell traveled for miles, and I believed it. A little while longer, the sprawling yard came into view.

I herded the horses into an empty corral and checked in with the office. After getting that business settled, I decided to poke around. I wasn't going to leave without having a word with Preston.

This was probably the busiest sale of the year. Everyone wanted to get their cattle and horses sold before winter, and buyers wanted to get their new purchases home for the same reason. I saw a few familiar faces and stopped to say a word or two here and there, but I didn't see any sign of Preston.

"Tucker!" A man shouted from behind me. I turned and was surprised to see the hulking frame of Thomas Tulley pushing his way through the crowd.

"Thomas." I clasped his hand and returned the smile of the big man. "It's been too long. What brings you to Kansas?"

"Thought I might try my hand in the cattle business."

I nodded. Thomas had worked with me in the territories out west. The last time I saw him, he was chasing around a pretty girl and thinking about settling down.

"You have land around here?"

"I have a place for now, but looking for something more permanent," he said.

"Well, you're always welcome in Colorado." Clint would be happy to have Thomas around too. Thomas was nearly as good-natured as Clint and strong as an ox. I don't know how an old gunslinger like me ended up with friends as good as Clint and Thomas.

"Colorado, eh? Is that where you settled down?"

"After my youngest was born, I just couldn't keep chasing the wind or the bad guys," I said. Mary had followed me out west. She tried to make a life there with the girls, but after Tuck Junior was born, she needed me more than I needed to be the hero of the West.

"How is Mary?" Thomas asked.

"She passed away a little over a year ago." My voice was rough, and I looked away from Thomas.

"I'm so sorry, Tucker. I had no idea. Some friend I am. It's really been too long."

"It has," I agreed. "Why don't you think about packing up and moving to Colorado? Clint's there too. It would be good for you. Good for us to have you around."

"I guess I'm still a drifter at heart," Thomas laughed. "Maybe Colorado will finally settle me down. I sure haven't found a woman that could do that yet." He laughed again and clapped me on the shoulder. It was like being swiped by a grizzly bear. I winced and rubbed my shoulder, which only made him laugh louder.

"You just need to meet the right woman," I said, and my eyes must have gone soft at the thought of Sierra because Thomas smirked at me.

"Have you found someone?"

I smiled, thinking about Sierra and how she came into my life. "I never thought I'd love anyone like I loved Mary. I wasn't looking for a woman, not really, but Clint urged me to put up a posting looking for a nanny for the kids. Then this woman came into my life and I...well, I haven't been the same since."

"I'm happy for you," Thomas said, and all teasing was gone. "I can't imagine what it must have been like for you and the kids to lose Mary. I'm glad you all have someone again. It's hard being on your own. Being alone."

"That's why you should move to Colorado." I caught the notes of wistfulness in my old friend's voice, and it bothered me to think of him struggling to make it on his own. There was no reason for him to go it alone when nothing was keeping him from moving closer to his friends.

"Okay, okay, you've convinced me. Maybe I should just drive my new cattle to your place and not set foot in the hovel I've called home for the last three months ever again."

"I've heard worse plans," I laughed. "But I have space for some cattle until you get settled. It's not a bad idea really. How many cattle you planning to buy?"

"How many you got room for?"

I shook my head and walked toward the main office. Usually, Preston was out mingling in the crowd, but I still hadn't seen him, and I wondered if I might find him in the office. Or maybe someone who knew where he was.

Thomas followed me inside, and his bulk took up most of the reception area in the tiny building. An older lady sat behind the desk, and I tipped my hat to her.

"Afternoon, ma'am. I was wondering if you knew where I might find Mr. McKlellan."

"I haven't seen him yet today, but if you head over to the auctioneer stand, sometimes he's around there. Or those boys over there might be able to direct you." She smiled at me, and I tipped my hat again.

"Thank you, I'll do that. You have a good day." I stalked out of the office and headed toward the stands. Thomas was still following me, but I could tell he had questions now.

"What are you doing looking for Preston McKlellan?"

"It's his auction, just wanted to ask him a few questions."

Thomas snorted. "I know you, Tucker. You don't ever just ask people questions. Especially not someone like Preston McKlellan."

I stopped in the road and Thomas nearly ran into me.

"What do you know about him?"

Thomas held up his hands. "Not a lot. Just that he's the richest man in the state of Kansas and probably the richest man in Missouri too. He's not a man you fuck with. Not even you."

"We'll see about that," I said.

Thomas sighed heavily, but I saw the gleam in his eye. He might try to talk some sense into me, but he wouldn't talk me out of anything. He always liked to see me bite off more than I could chew. And I planned to chew up Preston McKlellan and spit him out.

Sierra

C LINT SEEMED much better by morning, but I couldn't say the same for the barn. In the cold light of day, it smoldered and creaked and looked like it would collapse in the slightest wind. Still, we needed to see what we could salvage.

I had Annie helping the younger children with the washing since our clothes stunk to high heaven from all the smoke. Clint insisted he was okay to ride and wanted to find the missing mare. Storm had escaped in the night too, which seemed fitting considering everything else we had to deal with. He saddled Colonel without too much trouble, but he wobbled in the saddle once he was mounted.

"Are you sure you're up for this?"

"Have to be," he said with a grin, but it didn't have his usual goofiness behind it. "We need those horses, and I'm sure they haven't gone far."

"I wish Caroline could take a look at you." We had already discussed the doctor more than once, but Clint wanted to get the horses back first. Then he was open to figuring that out. We couldn't forget that there was still a reward out for me, and we were stuck between a rock and a hard place. On one hand, Clint could ride into town by himself, but that would leave me and the kids alone at the ranch. On the other hand, we could all ride into town, but then I had to show my face, and we wanted people to think about me as little as possible.

"I won't be gone long." He nudged Colonel into a walk and headed into the woods.

"You kids okay? I'm going to take a look in the barn." They nodded in response, and Annie gave the younger two an armful of wet clothes to hang on the line. It was cool this morning, but it would still be warm enough to dry our clothes before dark. Wet clothes were the least of my problems today, though.

I stepped carefully into the barn, mindful of the beams overhead and beneath my feet. It seemed about half had fallen and half still supported the barn. But I didn't trust them to stay that way. I hoped to salvage some of Clint's things and the remaining horse tack. Luckily, Clint had saved his saddle by throwing it in the wagon when we pulled it out.

I was dismayed to find most things burned beyond repair, but I still set all of Clint's clothes in a pile to sort through later. There might be something that could be saved or made into clothing for Tuck Junior. I was tugging a leather belt from under some fallen wood when I heard the fast footfalls of a galloping horse.

I assumed Clint forgot something, or maybe he had luck finding the other horses already. I didn't know why he was pushing his horse so hard though. I picked my way back through the burned barn as quickly as I could. I stumbled through the open door and nearly fell in the yard.

A horse thundered up the road to the house. I squinted into the sun. I couldn't tell who was on the back of the horse, but I knew it wasn't Clint.

I didn't even have time to scream for the children to get inside before the horse was bearing down on us. It tore through the yard and came to a sudden stop with a snort and squealing whinny. The rider fell from its back in a heap.

It was a woman.

My heart hammered in my chest, but some of my fear dissipated. I approached the rider slowly and

motioned for the children to stay back. They watched me
with wide eyes. Annie gathered the younger ones behind
her.

The rider moaned and stirred. She rolled over and
I gasped.

"Charity!" I breathed her name, not trusting that
what I was seeing was real. I reached down to touch her
face, and she blinked at me through swollen eyes. Her face
was bruised, and one eye was nearly swollen shut.

Ice filled my veins. A cold rage washed over me,
and my hands shook.

"Who did this?" I already knew in my heart, but I
needed to hear it from her. Tears leaked from her eyes and
left tracks down her cheeks.

"Preston," she said, and her voice was hoarse. I
could see her neck was bruised too, in a dark pattern of
purple fingers. "He's coming for you."

I got Charity into the house and laid her down on my bed.
The children gathered in the doorway, their faces scared
and curious. I gave them each a quick kiss on the tops of
their heads and asked Annie to get out the checkers to
entertain them.

"It's alright," I said, even though I didn't know if
anything would be alright. "Charity is a friend, and she's
just had an accident. Uncle Clint will be back soon." I

hurried into the kitchen for some rags and then ran outside to dunk one in the cold laundry water. Charity seemed more alert. She was staring at the ceiling when I returned. She still couldn't open one eye, but she turned to me when I paused in the doorway.

"Hey," she said, and a coughing fit shook her small frame.

"Shh." I moved beside her and gently pressed the cold cloth against her face. She hissed, but then relaxed under my touch. "How did you get here?"

"I heard Preston talking with Jackson. Saying how he was going to hunt you down and had a lead because of his posters. Preston caught me listening at the door." She paused and took a calming breath. "He...wasn't happy. Jackson wasn't happy with him for messing up my face, but Preston threw some coins at him and that was that. When Preston left, I went to the stable and took Jackson's horse. Maggie...what would we do without Maggie. She already had a bag packed. She planned to come, but after what happened, she knew I needed to get away.

"I'm done, Sierra. I'm never going back to Jackson. Anyway, Maggie gave me a map and I followed the train tracks most of the way here. I didn't think about what to do once I reached the town, but I ran into a nice lady... Caroline maybe was her name... and she directed me. I'm sure I look a mess. Must have scared her half to death."

"Caroline is a doctor." I dabbed at the cut over Charity's eye. "I wish she could have looked at you."

"She offered, but I had to get to you. I don't know how far out Preston is, but he's coming, Sierra." A sob caught in her throat and shook her body.

"Shh." I smoothed my hand over her head. "You rest. We'll be alright."

"Caroline...she said she'd follow me here," Charity murmured. I could tell she was exhausted, and I wanted her to rest. I hoped she was right about Caroline, though. It would be good to have the doctor visit today.

I closed the bedroom door behind me and looked out the front window. Everything seemed quiet for the moment. The children played checkers on the floor, and I hoped Charity would sleep. I needed to stay busy, but my mind couldn't focus. All I could think about was the fact that Preston was on his way here.

A horse whinnied outside, and I hurried to the window. Clint came into view, leading the missing mare and Storm. I flung open the front door and ran outside. If Preston was coming here, we needed to leave.

"Whose horse?" Clint's voice was rough, and he swayed in the saddle. I took the mare's lead rope from him and tied her to the hitching post.

"My friend. One of the girls from where I came from. She's in bad shape, and she brought bad news.

Preston is coming here." My words tumbled out, and I didn't know if Clint fully processed everything I was saying. The poor man looked dead in the saddle. I took Storm from him and was grateful the big horse was too tired to fight me. The stallion let me lead him back to his corral without any fuss. Clint was standing next to Colonel when I returned.

"We need to leave," Clint said. "Let's get the mare hooked up to the wagon. Shit, my head hurts." He leaned against Colonel's saddle.

"When will Tucker get back?"

"If the storm didn't catch him, tomorrow maybe." Clint frowned at the horizon, and I followed his gaze. It was quiet, and in the stillness, I could just make out the sound of horse hooves on the road. "Get inside."

Clint drew his shotgun from Colonel's saddle and followed me inside, never taking his eyes off the road.

"Charity said Caroline was going to come out; maybe it's her," I said.

"Maybe." Clint leaned against the wall beside the window, angling so he could see outside without being seen.

The children still played on the floor. I stood between them and the door, not sure what I was going to do, but determined to do what I could.

The rumbling of horse hooves got louder, but Clint

relaxed suddenly and stepped away from the wall. He opened the front door and motioned for me to follow.

"It's Caroline," he said as he stepped outside.

I let out a breath I didn't realize I was holding and hurried after him. I was so happy to see Caroline, I felt like crying. But I couldn't cry yet. Not until I knew Preston was six feet under. Even then, I wouldn't shed a tear for him.

I'd hold it all in until I could cry tears of happiness.

Tucker

I STALKED THROUGH the crowd.

"You going to tell me what your beef is with Preston?" Thomas asked.

"It's personal." I didn't mind telling Thomas the whole story, but I didn't have time for it right now.

"Gathered as much," he mumbled. Thomas probably would have said more, but we reached the auctioneer stand.

It was clear Preston wasn't around.

"He isn't here." I ground out the words through clenched teeth.

"We could ask one of those guys." Thomas pointed to some men in the auctioneer booth. I didn't want to talk to anyone else, but Thomas was already walking over and calling out to them. "Hey, fellas, you know where I might find Mr. McKlellan?"

The men exchanged a look and one of them smirked. The fat one with a smirk on his face opened his mouth. I knew I wasn't going to like his answer before he said a word.

"He had some business to attend to out West, but he should be around later. Tomorrow probably," the fat one said. The way he said 'business', I knew exactly what Preston was up to.

"He's a busy man." Thomas chuckled good-naturedly, and I was glad for his distraction. I was certain the look in my eyes was nothing less than murderous, and these men didn't need to get caught in my path. "I couldn't keep things straight if I was as busy as him. If I can leave here with a few head of cattle tomorrow, I'll count myself lucky."

"Got that right," the other man said. He was skinny and had a ratty beard sprouting from his chin. "Though I think he's had trouble himself with keeping things straight."

The fat man laughed. It wasn't a nice laugh, and I wanted to punch him in the gut.

"Reckon he'll get things straightened out soon

enough," the fat one said. "Usually doesn't take Preston long to get his whores back in line." Then both men were laughing, and I saw red. I took a step forward as Thomas spoke.

"Whoo boy, I know how that goes." Thomas gave me a seemingly playful shove that sent me sprawling out the door. I heard him talking to the men and making excuses about not knowing his own strength. I dusted off my hat and glared at the horizon.

"Thanks, I guess," I said when he came out the door.

"As much as I would've liked to see you beat the shit out of those two meatheads, this is not the time or place," Thomas said.

"I need to leave." I started back across the stockyard where I had tied Max. If I left now, I could make it to the ranch by morning. I didn't know when Preston had set out to find Sierra, or if he knew where she was. There was only one trail between here and there, so I might even catch him before he got there. I might also catch him as he was leaving my ranch, but I didn't want to think about that.

"Figured you'd say that."

"Can you collect my earnings and get yourself to my ranch with your cattle?" I handed Thomas the paperwork for my horses.

"Whatever you need. If you need me to come along, I have a good horse."

"No, I can handle this." I didn't want Thomas getting tangled up with Preston, too. Besides, Thomas was a big man, and even if he had a good horse, it wouldn't carry him all the way to Colorado at the speed I wanted to go. "Just take care of yourself and come to Colorado."

"You, too." Thomas shook my hand. "See you in a few days."

I mounted Max in a hurry and reined him out of the stockyard. He was a good horse, and I hoped he would put up with me driving him this hard. Soon, the auction was far behind us, and I alternated walking and trotting for a while.

"I'll make it up to you with lots of apples, boy." I patted his neck as I urged him faster. We both needed rest at some point, but with the flat plains of Kansas ahead of us, I wanted to make up as much time as I could.

Max's hooves pounded the hard trail and thundered through my whole body. We were going as fast as possible, but I wanted to go faster. I couldn't be too late. I couldn't. Not again.

I should have stayed at the ranch. I never should have left. I shouldn't have left Sierra this time, and I never should have left Mary.

Mary.

It was supposed to be one last job out West and then I was done, but the job took longer than planned. Mary caught the flu while I was away. A snowstorm came up, and my ranch hand at the time got stuck in town along with the doctor. I had come home to Mary and the kids sick as dogs.

Max carried me then, and I knew he would give it all he could. It wouldn't be his fault if we didn't make it. It would be mine. It was always mine.

"I'm coming for you, Sierra," I said the words aloud as if I could will myself to make it in time. I couldn't survive it if I didn't make it in time.

I had to save her.

I had to.

24

Sierra

CAROLINE FINISHED her examination and packed away her equipment in her bag. "I'd really like to get Clint to my clinic."

"We should all go," Clint said.

"I have room at the clinic. You can all stay until Tucker gets back, or as long as you need to," Caroline said. Since she already knew my story, it was easy to fill her in on Charity and the fact that Preston was headed this way.

Charity needed a few stitches in her head, but it had already been a few days since she received her injuries, so Caroline wasn't as concerned about her head wounds. Clint was still sluggish and slow to get around, so she wanted him to rest. Going to the clinic seemed to be the best option.

But I didn't want to put a target on Caroline too.

The kids were playing behind the house, and I was trying to pack and get things ready if...*when* we left. Guilt curled in my gut as I looked at Charity and watched the kids out the back window. I put a target on everyone the moment I chose this life. I should have known Preston wouldn't let me go. I should have known he would chase me to the ends of the earth.

And that he would find me.

Charity was sitting at the kitchen table. Caroline and Clint were near the fireplace. I sat by Charity and handed her a mug of coffee.

"Thanks," she said.

"How long do we have?" I whispered. I didn't want Clint and Caroline overhearing.

"Until Preston finds us?" Charity shivered, and she looked over her shoulder as if he might already be there. "I don't know, Sierra. He left me behind the saloon. I went out back to throw out some food scraps, and he followed. I guess he knew Jackson would never let him get away with this." She motioned to her face.

I clenched my fists to keep my hands from shaking. My body was nearly trembling with both rage and fear. Preston was always able to bring out both in me.

"Anyway, I didn't tell him anything, but he was going to beat me to death. Maggie came out. She had a gun, but so did he." Charity took a deep breath and blinked rapidly. "She told him where you went. She only did it to save me. I swear, she wouldn't have told him otherwise, but..."

"Shh." I put my hand over hers. "It's okay. I don't blame you or Maggie. I'm glad she saved you."

Charity nodded but didn't say anything.

"Well, I guess that gives us a little time, since he just has a town name and not Tucker's name. Still, I don't want the kids to be here when he comes."

"I'm not going back." Charity's voice was so quiet; I almost didn't hear her. "I don't want to be Jackson's girl anymore. I don't mind the work. There's a lot of men that are real sweethearts, but I don't want to work for Jackson anymore."

"Then you'll stay here with us. We'll get through this just fine, and we can both get our lives back."

She nodded at that, and I was pleased to see some of her fire coming back. Charity was always the spunky, over the top one. I knew part of it was for show, but I also knew she could burn brighter than any of us if she didn't have to live in Jackson's shadow.

Caroline joined us at the table. "Well, I've done all I can for Clint right now. We really need to get to the clinic. I'll feel better if everyone is out of harm's way and Clint can actually rest. He's on pins and needles here."

"What if we run into Preston in town?" Charity asked. It was a good point. I was thinking of Caroline's clinic as a refuge and completely forgetting about the fact that we had to go into town to get there.

Caroline didn't have an answer for that, and I felt the cold edges of fear start to grip my stomach again.

"We'll head out just before dark." I nodded to myself as if that settled everything, even though I didn't know how much time we had. Or if we had any time. "We'll take both wagons and space our arrival a little bit apart so no one will notice. Is Clint okay to drive a wagon?"

"Probably not," she shrugged. "But I doubt that will stop him."

"They'll be looking for me and Charity. If the kids ride with Caroline and Clint drives our wagon, we can lay down in the back and cover ourselves with blankets."

"Well, if that's the plan, then we don't have to wait until dark," Caroline said. "Clint can pull the wagon around behind the clinic. That's where I have wagons come anyway, so it won't arouse any suspicion. No one will ever see you."

"Do I hear you ladies makin' plans without me?" Clint asked. His tone was light, but I could tell he was exhausted. We all were.

"I'll get the horses hitched up." I stood and headed outside without waiting for anyone to say anything else.

I was hardly surprised when I got to the wagon and saw everyone had followed me outside.

"We can help," Charity said, and I rolled my eyes at her. "Well, I don't know the first thing about hitching up horses, but they can help, and I'll...I'll provide comedic relief."

I laughed at that. "Fine. If you want to help, get some food from the kitchen. It's nearly midday, and the kids will be hungry."

"Yes, ma'am," Charity said with a grin, and she disappeared back into the house.

Clint helped Caroline with her wagon first, though she kept insisting she could do it and he needed to sit down.

"You're whiter than a ghost," Caroline scolded him. "Sit down before you fall down."

"Yes, doctor." He tipped his hat as he slid into a sitting position against one of the porch posts. I brought up both mares, but I noticed the one that ran off was limping.

"Easy, girl." I tied the dapple mare to the hitching post and walked the bay one around the yard to see what was causing her trouble. "Clint, does she look like she's limping to you?"

He frowned at her and let out a long sigh. "Yeah, Tucker will need to take a look at her. I'd say put her in the barn, but..." he gestured at the still smoking structure. I led the mare back down to the smaller shed instead.

When I got back to the front of the house, Clint was trying to hitch the remaining mare to the wagon.

"Can she pull it on her own?" I only ever saw Clint use the wagons with both mares hitched to it.

"It would be nice to have both mares, but ol' Julie can manage on her own." He patted her neck and fiddled with the harness again. He let out a frustrated sound.

"What's wrong?"

"Was this tack in the barn?" he asked.

"Yes, there wasn't much that survived the fire. I picked through what was left this morning."

"That's fine. I'm glad you could save some of it, but it's mangled. I can make it work, but it will take time." Clint rubbed at his eyes and took the piece of harness to the back of the wagon. He grabbed some tools out of the wagon and started hammering on the piece of iron. I didn't know how long it would take, but time wasn't something we had much of.

"Let's go ahead and send the kids on with Caroline," I said. My heart hammered in my chest. A sudden urgency filled me, and I nearly ran into the house to get the children packed up. It was already past midday. By the time Clint found the horses and then Caroline arrived and looked everyone over, the day had just disappeared. I would feel better if I knew the children were safe. I would feel even better if Tucker were here, but I knew it was too soon to hope that he might show up. One more day, Clint had said, or maybe the day after. My days were all mixed up now, and I could barely remember when it was that Tucker rode out, let alone when he might return.

"Annie," I called out the back door where the kids were playing in the grass. "Bring your brother and sister and come inside. It's time to go into town with Dr. Morrow."

I threw some clothes in a bag and gathered the basket of food Charity had packed. Charity and Caroline waited outside while I herded the children out the door. I put the food and clothes in the back of the wagon and helped the kids climb in. Charity brought a quilt, and they snuggled in for the ride.

"We'll be right behind you," I told Annie. Then I kissed them each on the cheek and turned away before I started crying. My nerves were nearly shot, and I just wanted everything to be done and over. As long as it ended with Preston dead and everyone I loved alive.

"I'll take good care of them," Caroline said. I nodded, not trusting myself to talk. I felt like Caroline wanted to say some more words of encouragement, but such words were useless, and I think we all knew it. I was hoping for the best, but who knew how things would turn out.

"We'll be right behind you," Charity said.

Caroline climbed in her wagon and snapped the reigns. Her horse turned toward the road and the wagon ambled through the yard and bumped onto the road. I watched as they went. The children waved, as if they were on a big adventure. I raised my hand but couldn't bring myself to smile. I thought I would feel relief knowing they were headed into town, but dread pooled in my gut.

Clint was still hammering on the harness buckle. We were all packed and ready to go, and I had nothing left to keep me busy. Nothing to keep me from worrying about what was to come.

"Is there anything I can do, Clint?" I doubted I could help with repairing the harness, but I needed something to keep me busy.

"I think I've about got it now," he said. "If you want to check on Storm and the other horses real quick, that would give you something to do. They shouldn't need anything, but it's be good to check on them before we head out."

As I walked toward Storm's corral, I heard horse hooves on the road. I looked back at Clint. He already had the shotgun out of the wagon and laid across the seat. I hurried back toward the house as the hooves got louder.

"Get inside," Clint ordered.

I grabbed Charity and ran inside the house, but it wasn't just horses I heard. It was the jangle of a harness and the creak of a wagon. I stopped in the doorway and looked. Over the crest in the road, Caroline appeared with her horse and wagon.

I couldn't process what I was seeing.

"Why is she back?" I murmured.

"Maybe something happened to the horse?" Charity suggested.

But then another horse crested the hill. And another. Until there were four horsemen flanking Caroline's wagon. I didn't need to see their faces to know who led the horsemen. There was no mistaking the white horse or the dark figure of Preston McKlellan.

25

Sierra

AT THE SIGHT of the children and Caroline, Clint lowered his shotgun. I could hardly breathe as the horses came into the yard and Preston dismounted as if he owned the place. He was calm. Nothing about his demeanor suggested he was angry or even upset, but I knew him. When his eyes met mine, I saw the evil he hid so well.

The men with him were from town. The saloon owner, Harlan, and the two men that confronted Tucker when I first arrived. The one still had his leg in a splint from Tucker's bullet. I took a small amount of satisfaction when he got off his horse awkwardly and his leg nearly folded under him.

"Evenin'." Preston tipped his hat as if he just came over for Sunday dinner. "I believe we have some business to attend to. Let's take this inside, shall we?"

Then Preston waved everyone inside. I could tell Clint wanted to say something, but the girls were clinging to him. Caroline carried Tuck Junior. There was no room for anyone to be the hero with the children here, and Preston knew it.

I backed into the house as everyone came up the steps. I heard Charity scurry away behind me. I wondered if anyone saw her. She wasn't standing in the door with me, so maybe she could hide. There was no reason for them to know she was here.

My hope was short-lived. Preston scanned the house and immediately narrowed his eyes toward the bedroom door.

"Come on out," he said. "We're just gonna have a chat and then I'll be on my way."

A chill ran down my spine at his words. It was never just a chat with Preston. Someone always ended up hurt, or worse.

Caroline gathered the children to her by the fireplace. Clint was doing his best to stand up straight and not wobble on his feet, but he was barely holding on. Charity came out of the bedroom and Preston grinned.

"Can't say I'm surprised to see you here." He glanced around the house. "With two of Jackson's finest here, why, the proprietor could open his own saloon. Is that what you intended when you took Sierra from me?"

I jerked at Preston's words, realizing his focus was on Clint. He thought Clint owned this place. I didn't want Clint to take on anything else today, but before I opened my mouth, Harlan was already spitting out words.

"That's just the ranch hand. Reckon Tucker's off at that big auction in Kansas," Harlan said. Preston's jaw twitched and I could tell he wanted to put Harlan in his place. Preston never appreciated being corrected.

"Is that so?" Preston said. His words were smooth and deadly. "This man, Tucker...he's at my auction."

"Yes sir, Tucker West." Harlan bobbed his head in an eager nod.

"Tucker West." Preston's words were almost a question, and I saw a flash of something in his eyes I never saw before. It almost looked like fear, but I never saw Preston afraid of anything, so I must have been mistaken. He huffed out a little chuckle to himself and then glanced at his pocket watch.

The room was quiet, but Harlan and his men were restless. They shifted on their feet and paced around the kitchen.

"You men can go," Preston said. "I have everything under control."

"Go?" Harlan narrowed his eyes at Preston. "What about the reward money?"

"What about it?" Preston stared at Harlan and I knew he had no intention of ever paying the reward. "You didn't deliver Sierra to me, and your directions were passing at best, but I'm a generous man. For your troubles." Preston flipped a coin toward Harlan.

"The poster said $500." Harlan stepped toward Preston, and I stepped back in the same moment.

The gun shot filled the house with its sharp crack before I even processed that Preston pulled his gun. One of the girls screamed, but Caroline quickly shushed her.

"You shot me!" Harlan clutched his stomach with both hands. Blood seeped between his fingers. "You've killed me."

"You might still live." Preston motioned toward Caroline. "We have a doctor at our disposal, after all. Come, I believe this man wishes to live."

Caroline was shaking as she peeled the children away from her and moved toward Harlan. He slumped over in the floor, and I could hear his wet breaths.

Caroline examined the wound in Harlan's stomach. "I need the tools at my clinic." Blood pooled on the floor and soaked slowly into the dry wood.

"Load him in your wagon then," Preston said. "I have no use for him or you."

"Please, please help me, Doc," Harlan begged. He moaned and clutched at his stomach.

I saw Preston's hand move this time, but I still jumped when his gun went off. Harlan went still with a bullet between his eyes. I rushed to the children and tucked them against me. They trembled in my arms, and Gracie hiccuped quiet sobs into my skirts.

"Well, now, hopefully the rest of this business goes a little easier," Preston said. "You men want to leave?" He turned to Harlan's men. They shook their heads, but it was clear they wanted no more part in whatever Preston had planned.

"I'll go with you." My voice didn't waver. It hardly sounded like my own. The children gripped me tighter, but I gently pulled them away. Clint stepped closer, and they huddled around him. They watched me with wide, watery eyes. I gave them a small smile, then turned to Preston. "I'll go with you, and I won't cause you any problems." Just leave everyone alone, I wanted to say, but I knew better than to ask Preston for anything.

"Oh, Sierra, all you've done is cause me problems lately." He frowned at me, and I worried that he never intended to take me back. Maybe he just wanted to kill me to make me pay for leaving him. "Still, I have missed our nightly visits."

I nodded because I knew that was what he wanted. The movement was stiff, and his eyes glinted with dark amusement. I didn't know what he had planned for me, but I knew it was something awful. My throat closed up, and I felt lightheaded.

"Go on, then." He waved me toward the door. "It's a long ride to Kansas. We best get going."

My feet were wooden. I stepped toward the door, but it felt like the room was larger than before. I tried not to watch Preston's hands, but I couldn't help the way my eyes flicked to his gun. I waited for the shot, but it didn't come.

"You folks have a nice evening," Preston said, and then he was right behind me. His hand was on my back, pushing too hard and directing me outside.

I hardly breathed until Preston forced me up on his horse and mounted behind me. I was wedged between him and the saddle horn. His arms were like a cage around me. I wasn't thinking of myself, or my safety, as he spurred his horse to the east. The kids were safe. The kids were safe. This was my mantra as the horse thundered beneath us and the ranch fell away behind me.

In the dark, as Preston drove his horse through the foothills, the shock started to wear off and fear crept in. I was alone with Preston.

Tucker would find me. This became my new mantra as everything else faded away.

Tucker would find me.

26

Tucker

THE SUN HAD long since set by the time I finally reached the ranch. The moon was full, so I saw the horses and extra wagon in front of the house immediately. Max was coated in foamy sweat, and he breathed heavily. I slid off him quietly and unholstered my pistol.

Everything was quiet, but I didn't know if that was good or bad. I eased up along the house and stepped onto the porch. I stayed close to the wall and peeked in through the big window. The curtains were pulled, but I could see

Clint sitting by the fire through a small gap. His head was in his hands.

I didn't want to burst in on them and risk being shot, but I couldn't see the rest of the room or anyone else. Fire pumped through my veins, but my hand felt cold where I gripped my pistol. I had to know if the kids and Sierra were okay. I stepped toward the front door and nearly tripped on something large. In the shadow of the porch, the darkness concealed the body I kicked with my foot.

I sucked in a breath and knelt to get a look at the face.

"Harlan." I didn't know what went down here, but I needed to find out. I stepped over his body and pounded on the door. I heard hurried footsteps and the sound of a shotgun being cocked.

"Who's there?" Clint hollered.

"It's Tucker," I shouted through the door. Another hurrying of feet and someone said, "Thank the Lord."

The door opened, and I saw Clint illuminated by firelight.

"What happened?" I asked as I stepped into the room. "Where are the kids?"

"They're sleeping now," Clint said. I noticed his movements were slow, his steps heavy. He sat down again before I had hardly stepped into the room.

Caroline was in the kitchen. A younger woman sat

at the table. She was roughed up, and I wondered if she worked with Sierra. It made sense, but I didn't know why she was here.

"Where's Sierra?" I looked around the room, but she wasn't there. I hoped that she was sleeping too, but the grim faces told me otherwise.

"He took her," Caroline said.

"Preston?" I asked, even though I knew the answer. She nodded. "What happened?"

Caroline filled me in, but she didn't say anything about how Clint got injured. It was obvious something happened to him. She saw the question in my eyes when I looked at him, because she answered without me asking.

"Lightning struck the barn right after you left. It caught fire. Clint and Sierra were able to get the horses and wagon out, but a beam fell on Clint. I think he'll recover with some rest, but his head is pretty banged up."

I was hardly gone two days.

"Are the kids in the loft?" I stepped over to the narrow staircase, intending to check on them, but Caroline shook her head.

"They're in Sierra's room." She motioned toward the front of the house. I pushed open the door quietly. A tightness eased in my chest when I saw them all piled in the bed together, sleeping peacefully. Then I thought of Sierra, and the tightness came back tenfold.

"Why are there so many horses outside?" I figured

one belonged to Harlan, who clearly didn't need it anymore, but I couldn't figure out the other two.

"Oh." Caroline wrung her hands and looked to Clint.

"That's my fault." Clint barked out a laugh. "Made those two boys that were with Harlan walk back to town. Figured we can get Tuff to round 'em up later. I didn't want to keep watchin' them, but I didn't want them to have an easy go of it either."

"Which way did Preston go?" Max needed to rest, but there were plenty of horses outside. I was certain one of them could carry me.

The girl spoke for the first time "East. But he's not taking her back to Jackson. He said he will never let her out of his sight again."

Like hell. I clenched my jaw and felt the muscle in my temple pulse.

Now that I knew everyone else was safe, my focus was on Sierra. I had already let too much time pass. I swept out the front door, not even bothering to close it. I checked over the horses outside, but with a glance I knew they were all shit. One was lame, the other was overweight, and the third was nearly blind. Colonel was a sturdy horse but didn't have the speed I needed, and if I pushed Max now, he'd never recover. It might even kill him.

I yelled in frustration, and the horses shied away

from me. In the distance, the shrill cry of a stallion pierced the night.

Storm.

He was just green broke, but if any horse could catch Preston, he could.

"What are you thinking?" Clint asked. He stepped off the porch and followed my gaze.

"I'm thinking I have some killing to do." I pulled my saddle off Max's back and jogged to Storm's corral.

"Sounds about right," Clint said. He didn't follow me across the yard, but I knew he was watching. It was crazy what I was planning to do, but crazy was all I had.

And it had to be enough.

Sierra

M Y BODY ACHED from the harsh pace Preston forced his horse to take once we reached the foothills and the land started to flatten out. He pushed his horse for hours, and I could tell the beast was tired. Preston wasn't stupid. He had to know he couldn't keep pushing his horse like this. Not for so many miles and with two riders.

The horse stumbled and nearly went down. I lurched over the saddle horn, but Preston's iron grip kept me on the horse's back. Part of me wished I had fallen off. Maybe the horse would have trampled me, and it would all be over.

No, I couldn't think like that. Tucker would come. I knew he would. Maybe not in time to save me completely, but I knew he would find me.

"Damn horse," Preston growled. He jerked the poor animal to a stop, slid off the horse's back, and pulled me down roughly after him. "Get some wood for the fire." He shoved me toward some scrub brush, and I nearly fell. My legs were like jelly. The ground rolled beneath me after so many hours riding.

I didn't bother to argue with him or say anything. I limped toward the scraggly trees and searched the ground for dead branches. There weren't any big enough to use as a weapon. I returned a short time later with an armful of small branches and twigs.

Preston laid out his bedroll and cleared a small space to start a fire.

"Well go on, get the fire going. Aren't you a dutiful housewife now?" His voice was hard, and I was glad I couldn't see his eyes in the darkness.

I bristled, but my mind was tired and my body empty. I didn't have any words or smart comebacks, so I did as he wished and built up the sticks to start a fire. He stood behind me, watching everything I did. A sudden terror hit me, and my hands shook as I struck the flint and steel. Sparks showered the dry grass at the heart of the kindling. I blew gently over the embers, but I hardly had any breath. My chest ached and my hands were like ice.

I felt Preston move behind me. I jumped when his hard hand ran over my shoulder and through my hair.

"I've missed you," he said. I knew his words were true, but that didn't mean they were well-meaning. As the fire took hold, his hand suddenly fisted in my hair and jerked my head back. "You'll never leave me again. Come here." He hauled me up by my hair, and I scrambled to my feet, trying to ease the pull on my scalp.

He pushed me down opposite his bedroll and took out a length of rope. He roughly tied my hands and feet, then shoved me to my side. The fire was warm on my face, but my hands were cold where he pulled them behind me.

"You and me are gonna have a little chat in the morning," he said. Then he went to his bedroll, laid down, and pulled his hat down over his eyes. After a while, I could hear him snoring.

I wasn't completely immobile, but there was no way I could get out of the ropes or run while tied that way. I struggled a bit, but the rope rubbed my wrists and ankles. It only seemed to get tighter the more I tried to get loose.

I sighed and stared into the flames.

Tucker would find me. I believed it with my whole being, but I didn't know what would happen before he did.

I was surprised Preston stopped to rest, but he didn't really have a choice with his poor horse about to keel over.

The horse grazed a short distance away. Its flanks were lathered with sweat. Preston had taken the saddle and blanket off, but he didn't spend anytime wiping the steed down. Now I knew why he had a different horse nearly every week. It was always a white stallion, but I never saw the same stallion more than a couple times. I guess it made sense he rode his horses as hard as his women.

I nearly laughed at the dark thought but tamped down the urge. I blinked away the sudden moisture in my eyes.

I would kill him. The thought hit me like a sudden and profound truth. I glared at Preston's sleeping form across the fire and fell asleep thinking of all the ways I could end his life.

I woke to Preston's tall form staring down at me. He grinned when I met his eyes. I didn't like the way he looked at me.

I struggled to sit up. My body was sore from riding and from being tied up for hours. Preston grabbed my elbow and pulled me into a standing position. He moved behind me, and I felt him tugging at the ropes. Then I felt the cold steel of a knife against my wrist as he cut through the bindings. I heard the sleeve of my dress rip too. Preston chuckled unkindly.

"Oops," he said in a voice that told me it wasn't an accident at all.

I guess I should be happy my dress was the only

thing he cut. I pulled my arms around to my front, rubbed at my sore wrists, and rolled my shoulders.

"Sit," he ordered. Part of me wanted to stand defiantly, but my legs were sore, and the fire that filled me last night had dimmed in the cold light of morning. I sat heavily as Preston moved toward my feet. I thought of Tucker and the way he removed my shoes and stockings by the water. Preston grabbed my feet roughly, and all thoughts of Tucker's gentle touch disappeared.

Tucker and Preston were both dangerous men, but there was nothing else they shared. I couldn't see Preston for anything but evil. He fooled most people with his charm and flattery, but I had seen the other side of this man every day since I was fifteen.

"He'll come for you." The words slipped out before I even realized I spoke. Preston's eyes snapped to mine, and I saw that same flash of fear I saw at the ranch. Then it was gone, and his arrogant, hard look was back. But I knew what I saw.

Preston knew Tucker West, and he feared him.

"Then he's a dead man," Preston said, but the words didn't carry his usual edge. Knowing he feared Tucker made me bold.

"You're the dead man." I never would have spoken like that to Preston before, and his backhand reminded me why. My head snapped back as he connected with my jaw. As much as I wanted to stay upright, it wasn't possible.

My arms were weak and sore, and I barely caught myself. I was just glad I was sitting and didn't have far to fall.

I spat out blood, but I was not cowed by Preston's show of force. Maybe I should have been, and in my past life, I was. But I knew what life outside of the saloon was like now. I knew what life without Preston was like now, and it had changed me. When I looked at him, I felt fire in my veins. He saw it in my eyes and laughed.

"You think you can stand up to me now, is that it? You think you found yourself something better than me?" He leaned in and gripped my face painfully. "You'll never have anything better than me."

"I do." I said, though the words were painful to speak through his grip. His fingers were like iron pressing into my cheeks. "Tucker is better than you. In every way." I looked pointedly at his crotch hoping he knew what I thought about his small dick. I expected another backhand, but he laughed instead. It was a dark, cruel laugh. I almost wished he would hit me again instead of making that sound.

He searched my eyes, and I felt a bit of the old fear creep in.

"There she is." He ran his other hand through my hair. "I knew the scared little girl I claimed was in there somewhere. I think you've forgotten just how good you had it with me. And how good my dick is for you."

Preston unbuckled his holster and dropped it to the ground. Then he started unbuckling his belt. I tried to scramble away from him, but he was on me in a flash.

"Where you going, darlin'? I know you've been missing this, despite what you say. I know what you really want. I know what you need." I felt him grind against me. Even with the layers of clothing between us, bile rose in the back of my throat. He pressed me into the ground, one hand on my head. My ear smashed into the hard earth, and the rough grass scratched my cheek.

He grunted with the effort of holding me still and trying to get his pants undone. My own breaths were loud in my head. My arms flailed as the rest of me was held immobile by his weight. I trembled, and the ground seemed to tremble with me. No, it sounded like horse hooves pounding. The rumble of them traveled to me through the hard packed ground. I imagined it was Tucker coming to save me.

The thought stoked the fire inside me again. I moved my arms frantically, clawing at the ground and straining against Preston. My arm caught on something. I felt with my hand and found Preston's holster within reach.

I never liked guns before. Wouldn't even touch one, except when Preston put one in my hand when I was fifteen and dared me to pull the trigger. I dropped it like a hot iron back then. But now, with the hilt of his pistol so near my hand, I was not that same girl. I was still afraid, but I could save myself now.

I could barely see the holster with the one eye that wasn't crammed into the ground. Preston shifted his weight to pull at my skirts. I kicked at him while trying to move closer to the holster. I touched the gun but couldn't grip it.

Preston grabbed my waist and when he pulled me closer, he also pulled me closer to the gun. He hadn't given a thought to dropping the gun so close. He was so sure of my submission. So sure of my fear.

He was wrong.

My hand closed over the pistol, and I pulled it toward me. It caught in the leather, and I shook my arm to free it from the holster. It came out with one final pull, and I whipped it toward Preston wildly.

"What are you —"

BANG!

Preston exhaled harshly and sat back. His weight was off me enough that I scrambled into a sitting position. I aimed the gun at his heart.

"Fucking bitch," he said. He held his hands over the wound in his side. Blood seeped between his fingers, but it didn't seem like a lot of blood. I squeezed the trigger again, but Preston was faster than a snake. He knocked the gun away, and my shot went wide.

He wrestled the gun from my grip and staggered to his feet. He held the gun on me. His other hand still clutched his side.

"You'll pay for that." His breaths came heavy, but he didn't seem to be mortally wounded. The ground trembled beneath me. "A flesh wound, for a flesh wound." He aimed the gun at my arm, and I closed my eyes.

Tucker

STORM RAN LIKE the wind. It was like his hooves didn't even touch the ground when I let the reigns out and urged him to go. We covered the miles faster than I imagined, and he didn't seem to tire. After spending his days in the pasture, the stallion was ready to stretch his legs.

I rode east, hoping Preston was following the trail back to his auction. If he wasn't taking Sierra back to Missouri, then his stockyard was the only place I could think of that he would go. I hoped my guess was right. I didn't want to think about what would happen if it took me longer to find Sierra.

They had to be on this trail.

I reached the foothills and the land flattened out. If I thought Storm was flying before, then his speed became otherworldly on the flat ground.

"Good boy," I murmured, but my voice was swept away by the wind.

I leaned low over Storm's neck and strained to see any signs of Preston's tracks in the gray light of the coming morning. I squinted against the cold wind in my eyes and saw smoke in the distance.

A campfire.

It could be anyone, but my gut said it was Preston. His horse couldn't have traveled far with two riders, and I doubted any horse was as fast as Storm.

Dawn was coming, and I could see the hazy shadow of a horse in the distance. I saw one, maybe two figures near the fading smoke, but I couldn't be sure. I was too far away.

My fingers itched to draw my gun, but at this distance, even I couldn't hit anything. I didn't need to be much closer though.

Just a little closer.

Just a little more light.

Storm's breathing was finally growing labored. His sides heaved beneath me, but his steps were still sure. His heart was willing.

"Just a little longer, boy," I said — the words for

me as much as him.

The gray morning turned pink as the sun rose and finally, I could see the figures at the campsite. A white horse grazed, and a man and woman were on the ground nearby.

It had to be Preston and Sierra, but I couldn't be sure.

I drew my gun.

Storm's hooves were loud in my ears — his breaths harsh in the air.

A shot echoed across the flat ground. My gun came up on its own at the sound, but I needed to be sure who I was shooting.

The man stood, and at last I was close enough to see the woman too.

Sierra.

Preston held his gun on her, but I could tell he was wounded. Sierra must have shot him. I felt a warm pulse of satisfaction go through me, but now I could see the gun in Preston's hand. It was aimed at Sierra.

I didn't think.

I acted.

Years of taking down men like Preston flowed through my veins. I hardly contemplated shooting the man before I aimed and squeezed the trigger.

BANG!

Storm shied beneath me, and his steps faltered.

I nearly lost my seat but managed to stay on his back. Preston dropped like a dead weight, and I pulled Storm into a walk for the first time since we left the ranch.

Sierra scooted backward away from Preston's body and looked around wildly. Desperately. Her eyes met mine and I saw my name on her lips.

I jumped down from Storm's back and ran to her. I needed to know she was okay.

"Tucker!" Sierra cried when I was within arm's reach, and then she fell against me, clinging to me with everything she had. I held her just as tight. Over her shoulder, I saw Preston's body.

Dead.

My bullet between his eyes.

"Did he hurt you?" I held Sierra away from me so I could look at her.

"No ... not really, you got here in time." She pushed hair out of her eyes and her hand trembled slightly. Her wrists were raw and I caught her hand gently to look. I wanted to take her at her word, but I couldn't help but notice the rips in her clothing, and the scrapes on her cheek. Her lip was split and a bruise was forming high on her cheek bone. She fidgeted nervously under my gaze and I shifted my focus back to her wrists.

"These need tended to."

"It's fine, just a little rope burn," she said. "I'm okay, now that you're here and he's ... dead." She shivered. I pulled her against me again.

"You shot him," I said, and she nodded against me. "That's my girl."

She laughed at that, burrowing into my embrace. I held her tighter and buried my face in her hair. We needed to get back to the ranch and send Tuff out to deal with this, but for the moment, I didn't want to let her go.

"Thank you," she said. "For saving me."

"I reckon you were well on your way to saving yourself, but you know I can't resist playing the hero when I get the chance." I grinned at her, and she laughed softly again.

"You're not playing at anything. You are a hero. My hero." When she looked up at me shyly through her long lashes, a fire burned through me hot and urgent. I descended on her mouth like a starving man, and she met me like a woman possessed.

I would have made love to her right there, courting be damned, but Preston's presence even in death — *especially* in death — ruined the moment.

"Come on." I pulled away from her reluctantly. "Storm's done, but we can take Preston's horse and head back." At the mention of Preston, Sierra went rigid. I led her away from the campsite and his cooling body.

I lifted Sierra up onto the bare back of the horse and mounted behind her. The bridle was still on, so I took the reins and urged the horse toward Storm. The black stallion was worn out, but an easy walk would do him good, and I knew of a spring nearby where we could all rest.

Sierra melted into me as we rode. Her body rocked against me with every step of the horse, and I couldn't help but pull her even tighter against me. I wrapped one arm around her waist and she covered my hand with her own. I leaned in and kissed her neck. She shivered against me.

We reached the spring, and I helped her dismount, then I tied the horses a short distance away where they could graze and drink spring water. I took Sierra's hand and walked down to the water. I was reminded of the last time we went to the water together. When I met Sierra's eyes, I knew she was remembering that day too.

Her eyes were like liquid fire. When we kissed, the heat of it touched my soul. We came together like a spark and dry tinder. I couldn't get enough of her soft skin and gentle curves. Easing her down into the soft grass near the water's edge and settling between her thighs felt like coming home. I told myself to take things slow, but the adrenaline from our recent danger had me shaking with need.

"I don't ever want to lose you again." The thought of losing her had nearly killed me. I wanted her with me for the rest of my life. "I love you, Sierra."

Her eyes welled with tears. I gently wiped away a tear as it spilled from her eye.

"I love you too, Tucker West." Her breaths were ragged and her chest heaved against me where our bodies were pressed together. "I need you. All of you."

My nostrils flared at her words. "I promised to court you right. You deserve so much more than what I can give you. You deserve the world."

"I want you. Please."

Her words nearly made me come undone, but we were both emotional and I needed her to know how much she meant to me.

Everything.

"Sierra Sutton I never thought I'd meet a woman like you. You make me feel things I'd given up on feeling again. Will you do me the honor of marrying me?"

29

Sierra

I KNEW TUCKER intended to court me, but still, hearing him propose was a shock — a glorious shock. I gaped at him and when his brows furrowed at my lack of response, I forced the answer past my lips.

"Yes." The sound tore out of me more sob than word and Tucker's face broke into a grin.

"Yes?" He searched my face as if looking for any sign that he misheard or I misspoke.

"Yes," I said again and my voice sounded far more steady.

Tucker descended on me, but this time when our lips met there was less urgency — less desperation.

But the need was still there.

The hunger.

I tugged at Tucker's belt and he sat back to give me better access.

"You're beautiful." His eyes followed the same path as his hand as he caressed my face, then traced feather-light fingers along my neck before resting firmly on my breast. His eyes darkened as he rubbed his thumb over the fabric covering my hard nipple. I gasped at the sensation and he smirked devilishly.

His hands stilled mine where they struggled with his belt.

"Let me take care of you." His words were gruff with desire. He quickly removed his belt but didn't take off anything else. Instead, he moved his hands to the front of my dress and began the delicate task of undoing the tiny buttons there. His knuckles brushed my nipples as he worked and the sensation sent a jolt of electricity straight through me. I clenched my thighs where he still knelt between them and he chuckled low in his throat. I ran my hands under the back of his shirt as he worked and marveled at the expanse of hard muscles.

He loosened the last button and my breasts sprung free, now covered only by the paper thin material of my chemise. Tucker growled low in his throat and descended on my breast, gently biting my nipple through the fabric.

"Tucker," I gasped his name and he hummed against me. I needed to feel his mouth on my skin. Apparently he felt the same, because in the next moment he slipped my dress and chemise from my shoulders, shoving them down to my waist. My nipples hardened even further as the cool fall air swept over me. Tucker sat back and looked at me. He didn't try to hide the way his eyes took in my body and while the look in his eyes was exhilarating, I also suddenly felt self-conscious lying in the grass naked from the waist up. I moved my arms thinking to cover myself, but Tucker caught my wrists lightly, ever careful of the raw skin there.

"You're beautiful," he breathed again, and I felt my face flush. "I like looking at you. If that's alright?"

His words caused a rush of warmth between my legs and I couldn't help but nod as I let my arms relax.

"I'd like to look at you too," I whispered, and he gifted me with that devilish grin again.

"Well now, that only seems fair." He moved his hands to the buttons on his shirt and I reached up to help him. His eyes never left my breasts as he worked, and I'd never been more aware of that part of me in my life. My chest rose and fell with every breath I took as my nipples pebbled into hard points, begging for his mouth.

At last his shirt came undone and I shoved it back off his shoulders. I only had a moment to admire the view before Tucker leaned forward to claim my breast. He nipped and sucked eagerly, and I arched toward him, urging him to take whatever he wanted — whatever he needed.

But he didn't just take — he gave.

I'd never imagined such pleasure as he rolled my nipple gently between his teeth. With a final tug, he moved from one to the other as his hands danced along my sides.

I dug my short nails into his back, straining to pull him closer.

Heat and liquid throbbed at the juncture of my thighs. I needed more of him.

I needed all of him.

I tugged at his waistband then reached between us to unfasten his pants.

Tucker must have felt the desperation — the need — in my movements. He raised up for a moment and somehow pulled my dress off and shoved his jeans down in two quick movements.

Only my chemise, now bunched at my waist and barely covering the apex of my thighs, shielded me from his view.

My instinct was to hold the chemise in place and clamp my thighs closed, but the sight of his arousal made me bold. I gazed up at him through heavy eyes and slowly inched the hem of my chemise higher until the thin garment banded my waist and I was bare to him.

His calloused hands were deliciously rough and warm as he raked them down my body. Skimming over my sensitive nipples, skirting along the soft flesh of my belly and then coming to rest on my thighs.

He watched me with hunger in his eyes and the intensity of it had me squeezing my legs together but he held them open with gentle, but firm hands. Then he pressed them even farther apart as he scooted down and leaned in to kiss along my inner thigh.

I'd never been touched like that before and I squirmed under him.

"Wait," I gasped and he immediately stilled. His eyes met mine and his brow furrowed. Worry clouded his gaze as I bit my lip. "Don't you need..."

"This isn't about what I need," he growled. Then he squeezed my thighs and pulled me closer. "But if you want me to stop..."

Did I want him to stop?

"No." I felt my face flush, this time with something bordering on embarrassment. "I've just never ... no one ever ..." My eyes darted between his lips and where I still lay spread bare before him.

Realization cleared the confusion on his face and his eyes flashed with excitement.

"Let me take care of you," he growled as he descended on me once more. He nuzzled along my inner thigh until he reached my center.

I gasped.

Warmth spread through me, pooling where his rough tongue smoothed over my aching flesh.

"Tucker," I cried out and he growled deep in his throat. His hands clenched my thighs, pressing me even closer than I thought possible.

I fisted my hands in his hair as his fingers joined his mouth and the sensation sent me over the edge.

I cried out as waves of pleasure thrummed through me and Tucker licked and kissed his way back up my body until he was stretched over me and I could feel his hard length pressing against me.

"I need you." I angled my hips and wrapped my legs around him.

He groaned as he pressed against my entrance and I couldn't believe how complete and whole I felt as he thrust deep inside me. I had never experienced something that felt so right. So perfect.

"Tucker," I gasped and he stills inside me.

"Are you alright?" His eyes search mine and I could feel him trembling as he held himself back.

"Wonderful," I grinned and he returned the look, his dimples sending a new wave of warmth through me.

He moved slowly at first, but I wanted more and I could feel the tension in him as his body demanded more too.

"Harder," I whispered in his ear and he growled as though I had given permission for him to release some wild part of himself.

He set a hard and fast rhythm, and it was perfectly rough. My breasts bounced with every thrust and his eyes were nearly black with desire as he watched me. His hands gripped my hips as he brought me against him again and again. I rocked my hips to meet him as my belly tightened each time he thrust himself deep inside me. As his breath quickened, he reached between us and his thumb worked the most sensitive parts of me. Lightning shot through me and I felt myself fall over the edge. The world beyond ceased to exist. My awareness consisted only of his warm hands and the fullness inside me.

My body trembled with pleasure, and Tucker cried out as he filled me. He collapsed on me, and I relished the heavy, warm feel of him. I ran my hands over the broad expanse of his back. His weight was the sweetest burden I had ever felt. I nearly whined when he lifted some of his weight off me.

I almost felt guilty for feeling so good in this moment. Part of me thought I should feel bad that Preston was dead, but I didn't. There was nothing inside me that regretted his death. And nothing inside me regretted what I just did with Tucker so soon after my ordeal.

We needed each other.

We would be back to the ranch by the end of the day, and then there would be no time for anything except telling the sheriff what happened and taking care of the kids, Charity, and Clint. So, I wasn't going to feel guilty about the moment we shared.

I was going to treasure it.

I would treasure every moment with Tucker. Every word. Every touch. Every kiss.

Because Preston had nearly taken all that away from me.

I knew I couldn't survive without Tucker. The thought that I needed a man as desperately as I needed Tucker would have scared me before, but now it filled my heart because I knew he needed me as much as I needed him.

Tucker helped me dress and then we gathered our things and readied the horses. He pulled me in close and dropped a gentle kiss on my forehead before helping me onto the white horse.

I was ready to be home.

Home.

I smiled at the thought and caught Tucker's eye.

"What's going on in that pretty head of yours?" Tucker asked as we rode the horses toward the foothills. Storm recovered enough to carry Tucker, but even on separate horses, there was still not much space between us — Tucker kept bringing Storm in close every time we started to drift apart.

"Life," I said. "Our life...together."

"That's a good thing to think about." He smiled at me, and I thought what a sap I was. He had me going weak at the knees every time I saw that smile, the dimples that only showed up on his cheeks when he smiled, the way his eyes crinkled.

He was the most handsome man I ever saw, and he was mine.

"You keep lookin' at me like that and we'll have to find another spring," he said. I couldn't help the laugh that bubbled up inside me.

"That's not necessarily a bad thing," I said. "I'm sure the horses are thirsty."

"So am I," he growled, and the thrum of his voice shot straight to my core. He pulled our horses together so they were touching, then reached over to cup the back of my head. Tucker leaned in and captured my lips with his own. It was a hungry kiss, but he gave as much as he took, and I took it all.

"We'll never get back to the ranch at this rate," I murmured when we broke apart.

He shrugged. "I can't say that I care at the moment."

"We have forever together," I said, and that thought filled me with such hope that my heart felt like bursting.

"Forever might not be long enough," Tucker said. "For all the ways I want to show you I love you."

I blushed at his words, even as heat pooled in my belly. His gaze was heated, but he seemed to come back to the moment in a rush and shook his head.

"We should get back to the ranch." He sighed and squeezed my hand as he put a little more distance between the horses. "But we're going to send the kids into town to stay with Mrs. Grady for a night or three as soon as things are settled."

"I'm counting on it," I said, and he gave me a wicked grin.

"I bet you are." He waggled his eyebrows, then urged Storm into a faster walk.

I was more eager than ever to get back to the ranch and settled into our life together. I thought life with Tucker was good before, but with the threat of Preston gone forever, I felt like I was getting a fresh start all over again. I was getting a good life with a good man, and there was no one that would take that away from me.

Tucker

THE SUN HAD set by the time we rode into the ranch. Sierra was nearly falling asleep, and both the horses were dragging. I was feeling the effects of the past days' events, too. First driving the horses to auction, then racing back home and chasing down Preston.

It was a lot, even for me.

I was out of practice with this sort of thing, and I couldn't say that I missed it. I put that life behind me, and recent events reminded me why.

I was still good at killing, but I didn't like it.

There had been a time when ridding the world of another evil man made me fly higher than the clouds. I felt relief that Sierra didn't have to worry about Preston anymore, but I also felt the weight of his death on me in a way I never did before. It wasn't up to me to rid the world of evil. I would protect my family to the ends of the earth, but if I needed a reassurance that I chose the right path by hanging up my pistols, Preston's death was it. I was thankful my family was safe, thankful Sierra was safe, but I wasn't itching to ride out again anytime soon.

Clint was sitting on the porch when we rode up.

"Shouldn't you be at the clinic?" I asked. He looked better than when I left, but he still didn't look good.

"I can rest here same as at the clinic," he grumbled.

The front door flew open, and the kids rushed out of the house. They were talking all at once, and I dismounted to grab them up in my arms. I released them for a moment to help Sierra down, and then they were piling on her too.

"Easy, kids." I pulled Sierra toward me to brace her against their overzealous attentions. "Is the doctor still here?" The kids nodded, and I shooed them back inside. We followed, Clint limping along behind us.

Caroline and Charity met us at the door. We could hardly get inside before they were hugging Sierra and then hugging me too.

"Did anyone send for the sheriff?" I asked.

"I rode into town earlier, but he was out," Caroline said. "I left a message with his deputies, and they said he'll come out just as soon as he gets back."

"You see any sign of Harlan's men?"

Caroline shook her head. Clint and I never would have left loose ends like that in the past, but I trusted Tuff to wrap things up for us. I wasn't about to go hunt them down.

"I delivered Harlan's body to the sheriff's office, too."

"Thank you." That was one less mess to clean up. I noticed the floors had been scrubbed again, and the blood was hardly noticeable anymore. "We've all had a long day. I think it's about bedtime for everyone. Let's hope Tuff shows up in the morning." I kissed the kids good night, and after hugs and kisses from Sierra, they climbed the ladder to the loft.

"What happened with Preston?" Charity asked once the kids were out of earshot.

"He won't be bothering anyone anymore," I said.

"What about Jackson?" Sierra looked at Charity. The younger woman flinched at his name, but then she gathered herself and stood up straighter.

"I'm not going back," she said.

"I already told you, you're welcome to stay here," Sierra said. She looked at me quickly.

"Of course, whatever you need. We'll help you get settled in here," I said. I wasn't about to turn the poor woman out, especially when it was likely Jackson would be coming for her.

Maybe I hadn't hung up my pistols completely, because the idea of shooting another man like Preston suddenly sent a spike of satisfaction straight through me. I shook my head to clear the thought. I supposed shooting a man that came looking for trouble wasn't the same as hunting a man down and taking the trouble to him.

"There's room in the barn temporarily," I said, and Clint and Sierra looked at me like I had two heads. "What?"

"The barn's gone. It got burned up by lightning," Clint said.

"Oh, I forgot." I had yet to see the ranch in the daylight since my return, and the extent of the damage hadn't exactly been on my mind. "We'll figure out something..."

"You can stay with me," Caroline said. "It's no problem. And if you'd like a job, I always need an extra hand at the clinic."

Charity looked to Sierra, who nodded in encouragement. "Okay, I'd like that. Thank you."

"Well, that's settled. Now, if I could just get your bull-headed ranch hand to come into the clinic, I'd feel much better about everything." Caroline pinned Clint with a withering look.

"I'm fine. I don't need you hovering. I'll sit and I'll rest, and I promise not to do anything that could get me hurt for at least a week." Clint put a hand over his heart.

"Fine," Caroline huffed. "I need to get back to town. Charity, would you like to come along tonight?"

Charity nodded, and I went outside to help with the horses and wagon.

"I'm sorry I wasn't here," I said to them once they were in the wagon.

"None of this is your fault, Tucker," Caroline said. "Everything worked out, and that's what we should focus on."

"Can you go by the sheriff's office on your way home?" I gave Caroline directions to tell the deputies where Preston's body was. Something might have dragged it off by now, but at least I could say I tried to get his body back. "Do you need me to follow you in?"

"We'll be okay, Tucker." Caroline patted my hand. "You just take care of your family. I promise we'll go straight to town, and we'll stay on the road."

"Makes me nervous, you ladies riding out at night alone." I didn't want to get back on a horse, but I couldn't stand the feeling that they were unprotected.

"They won't be alone," Clint grumbled as he

stomped down the porch stairs. He had a shotgun and blanket with him. He set both in the back of the wagon and heaved himself up. "I don't have anywhere to sleep anyway. Reckon I might as well sleep at the clinic." Caroline ducked her head to hide a smile, and I shook my head.

"Be safe," I said. "Don't give the good doctor too much trouble, Clint." He grunted in response, and I chuckled. It felt good to have things getting back to normal.

"Reckon I can light a fire under Tuff's ass too," Clint said, and then I did laugh because Clint had never lit a fire under anybody's ass.

"You do that." I was still chuckling as the wagon disappeared down the road.

Sierra was sitting by the fire when I went back inside the house. I could tell her thoughts were far away as she looked into the flames. I thought I should do something to bring her back to the present. The shock of everything was settling in, but I wanted her to remember where she was and that it was over. She was safe.

"What if Jackson comes?" she asked.

"Let him come," I said. "I'll put a bullet in his head too...Or maybe you will. You don't have to fear any man ever again, Sierra."

She nodded, but her gaze was unfocused, her

thoughts still somewhere in the past...or the future. The only future I wanted her thinking about was the one we were going to make here with the kids.

"You and Charity are safe here. I promise." I couldn't help the twinge of guilt that reminded me Preston took Sierra. I promised her she was safe, and then he took her.

"What are you thinking about?" she asked.

"I promised to keep you safe, and I didn't."

"You saved me," she said. "You can't keep me in a bubble, Tucker, but I know you'll always protect me."

"I'll ride to the ends of the earth for you." And it was true.

"On Storm, you probably could," she smiled.

"You're right about that." I'd been debating whether to keep the stallion, but after his performance, I would be crazy to sell him.

"After we talk with Tuff, let's just put it all behind us. I need to move on," she said quietly.

"If that's what you want." I didn't want her to bottle everything up, but I understood wanting to leave the past in the past. "I'm always here for you. Whatever you need."

"Right now, I just need you," she said. Her voice was raw with emotion and desire.

"If that's what you want, I can help with that too."

I leaned in, and when our lips met, it was not the raw, hungry passion of earlier, but a deep, gentle promise of forever.

1881

Epilogue

Sierra

Six Months Later

I GROANED AS I lifted the heavy iron pan out of the pot belly stove. My arms strained with the weight as I held it away from my growing belly. I set the golden cake on the wooden counter to cool. My stomach rumbled as the buttery smell filled the kitchen.

"Are you going to love sweets as much as your brother?" I rubbed a hand over my taut stomach and felt the life within me kick. I chuckled. "I'll take that as a yes."

"How's Junior doing?" Tucker came up behind me and wrapped his arms around my stomach. I placed my hands over his, and the morning sun glinted off the small stone in my wedding ring. I never got tired of looking at that ring, or his either.

"You already have a Junior," I teased him.

"Fine, then how's Junie doing?" He kissed my neck, and I could feel the smirk on his face.

"She's fine. Seems to be as excited about cake as everyone else in this family. That sweet tooth must come from your side."

"Mmm, cake," Tucker murmured into my neck. "I can think of something else my sweet tooth would like to have this morning."

I laughed and pulled away from him. "Oh, stop! You had plenty of sweets last night, and we have a party to get ready for. It's not every day a girl becomes a teenager."

"Don't remind me," Tucker grumbled. He couldn't seem to accept that Annie was turning thirteen.

"Go on. I know you have a present to wrap." I shooed him from the kitchen.

"I'd rather unwrap something," he said with a wicked grin and a tug on my apron, then he was out the door and headed to the barn.

I laughed as I watched him walk across the yard. It was good to see the ranch looking whole again, with the barn rebuilt and the corral expanded with a new chute for working cattle. The arrival of Tucker's friend, Thomas, and a hundred head of cattle was a surprise to everyone but Tucker. It turned into quite the blessing, having that bear of a man and his cattle show up when they did. With Thomas's help, the barn was nearly erected overnight, and nobody was complaining about the addition of beef to our menu.

Clint was setting up a table in the yard and Thomas was putting the finishing touches on some yard games. Caroline and some other people from town, along with Annie's friends from school would be arriving any time now.

Annie came through the front door, her face flushed with excitement. She wasn't one to want to be the center of attention – that role was reserved for Tuck Junior – but I could tell she liked all the attention today.

"Is that my cake?" Annie tried to peek around me, but I steered her away from the kitchen.

"I have something for you." I led her toward my old room. It was empty since Tucker and I were married, but I thought it was time to change that. "Well, two somethings actually. First, your dad and I think it's time you had your own space." I opened the door to her new bedroom.

Annie gasped as she took in the redecorated room. Caroline and Charity had made a quilt for the bed. Thomas had built a little chair which sat by the window.

In the corner, a round table built by Clint held a small oil lamp, a quill and ink, along with a small diary.

"This is all for me?" Annie asked after I finished telling her about all the new gifts in her room. "Everything is so beautiful. Thank you!" She threw her arms around me, and I held her close.

"Caroline and Charity can't wait to see your room," I said. Those two had jumped on the chance to make a quilt when we told them our plans for the room.

"But where will the baby sleep?"

"In our room." I smoothed her hair and kissed her forehead. "And when the baby is big enough, he or she will join your siblings in the loft. Or maybe your dad will have added on to this house by then."

"I bet Thomas could build us a whole house in a day!" Annie said.

I laughed. "I bet he could."

Annie looked at her room again, and this time she noticed the dress at the foot of the bed.

"What's this?" She picked up the dress and ran her fingers over the silk.

"That was mine when I was about your age," I said. "My mother made it for me, and I thought you might like to have it."

"It's beautiful." Annie held the dress up, and I couldn't help the tears that gathered in my eyes. I remembered my mother working on that dress in our tiny room at the saloon. She befriended the seamstress who made all the girls' dresses, and the woman gave her every scrap of silk and lace she had left over. It was like a beautiful quilt, the pieces perfectly matched by color and size so that you wouldn't know it wasn't planned that way to start. The sleeves were long and full, with lace at the wrists and high neckline. The skirt brushed the floor in layers and layers of multi-colored silk. It was a dress for special occasions, but it wasn't gaudy despite the many colors.

It was a dress for a lady.

A dress for the woman my mother hoped I would become.

A dress for someone who would one day be loved and cherished.

It had been the perfect gift for me, and now it was the perfect gift for Annie.

"Can I wear it today?" Annie twirled with the dress held against her, and the skirt fanned away from her.

I laughed, "Of course you can wear it today. I hoped you would like it."

"I love it," she said. "Thank you."

Outside, we heard the jingle of horse tack and creaking of wagons. The shouted greetings let us know the party guests had arrived. I hurried outside while Annie quickly changed in her room.

"How'd she like the room?" Tucker pulled me to him as I stepped off the porch.

"How do you think she liked it?" I laughed. "She loved it."

He nodded at that, and we greeted Caroline, Charity and all the others as they clambered down from their wagons to started unloading baskets of food and treats.

"I smell pie," Tucker said, and he hurried to help Mrs. Grady with her baskets.

Everyone applauded when Annie stepped out of the house. Her friends fluttered around her like a flock of hens as they admired her dress.

I looked for Tucker, wondering what he thought of his little Annie in her new dress, but I didn't see him. I frowned as I searched the crowd of people, but then Clint directed everyone's attention to the barn with a piercing whistle. I smiled, realizing where Tucker was. I watched as Thomas rolled open the heavy barn doors, but as soon as Tucker stepped out, I shifted my gaze to Annie.

I didn't need to watch Tucker lead the little pinto out of the barn. I had already seen the horse a dozen times, and we were all waiting to see Annie's reaction to the pretty filly.

It was worth it.

Annie squealed and started hugging everyone she could reach. She jumped onto the porch and threw her arms around me, then bounded back down the steps. She took off at a run across the yard but slowed to a walk before she was too close to the horse. She squeezed her dad until I thought he might turn blue, then turned to the horse almost shyly. She held her hand out for the filly to sniff, and I could see the pride in Tucker's eyes at how good Annie was with the animal already.

Tucker had braided the horse's mane and tied off the braids with little pieces of twine. He had asked me for a piece of ribbon days ago, and now I saw he had braided the horse's tail and tied it up with a pretty silk bow.

He grinned at me over Annie's head, and I couldn't help the happy tears that gathered in my eyes.

I leaned against the porch and smiled at the gathering of friends and family. I never felt more surrounded by love in my whole life. I ran a hand over my stomach, enjoying the feel of the growing life inside me. This new life didn't seem real.

But it was.

And it was all mine.